DATE		

The Killing Circle

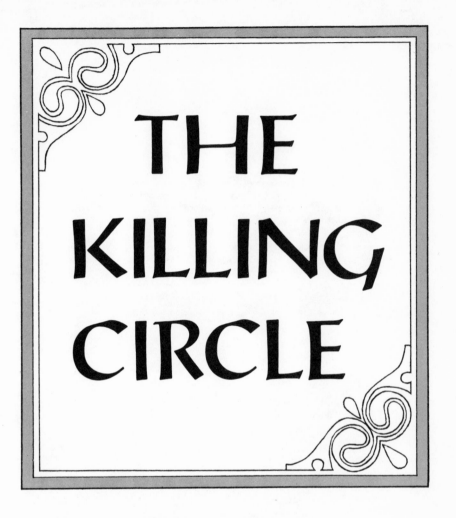

THE KILLING CIRCLE

by CHRIS WILTZ

MACMILLAN PUBLISHING CO., INC.
NEW YORK
COLLIER MACMILLAN PUBLISHERS
LONDON

Macmillan Publishing Co., Inc.
866 Third Avenue, New York, N.Y. 10022
Collier Macmillan Canada, Inc.

Library of Congress Cataloging in Publication Data

Wiltz, Chris.
 The killing circle.

I. Title.
PS3573.I4783K5   813'.54   81-13648
ISBN 0-02-630150-4   AACR2

10   9   8   7   6   5   4   3   2

Printed in the United States of America

To Ken McElroy

Contents

Special thanks to Patrick Bishop, Eddie "Mac" McLaughlin (retired, New Orleans Police Department), and Clare Leeper

If you have form'd a Circle to go into,
Go into it yourself and see how you would do.

—WILLIAM BLAKE

The Killing Circle

1

Fathers and Sons

WHENEVER THE OLD MAN POPS A BEER at seven in the morning, things are off to a bad start.

Every once in a while I get what is a sort of homesickness and run over to my parents' house in the Irish Channel for breakfast. My mother and Mrs. Tim, her next-door neighbor, had already finished hosing down their steps and galleries, since even at this hour the day promised to be a typical New Orleans scorcher. It's this early morning Channel bustling I miss. Children born in the suburbs remember summer days and the sounds of lawn mowers. The sounds of my childhood are hoses on the verandas.

The front door on my parents' side of the double was open but the screen was latched. As I went around to the back, I could hear the kids, my sister's kids, screeching through the shotgun rooms. Reenie, who lives with her husband in the other half of the double, had probably gone back to bed. I sympathize with the old man for having to take noise at this pitch so early in the morning. And this was August, the third month of no school, so undoubtedly he was under a lot of pressure. For that matter, he could have been on his way to the refrigerator, but I think it was the sight of me in the kitchen doorway that set him in the direction of the beer.

He was running around in his U-shirt and shorts and he grunted when he saw me.

My mother, on the other hand, was glad to see me. She immediately started pouring coffee, frying more bacon, and catching me up on the family news. Reenie was pregnant with her third, but according to my mother's logic, this was okay, since Michael had passed his test and was now a full-fledged sergeant in the New Orleans Police Department. It was out before she could stop it. The old man came alive.

"Yeah, ain't that somethin', Neal? Just think, you could be a lieutenant by now," he said. My mother rolled her eyes heavenward. I knew she was praying. I wished I had gone to the Hummingbird for breakfast.

"That's somethin', alright, Dad. Good for Michael."

He was all puffed up. "Yeah. Came in right up at the top of the class. Third, wasn't it, Mama?" Ma nodded and put breakfast on the table.

"So how's Reenie feeling?" I asked. The old man wouldn't be diverted, but all I needed was enough time to bolt breakfast before he started in earnest.

Ma was quick. "Oh, the poor darlin', Neal. She's just as sick as can be every mornin'. She waits until I finish up with breakfast and then comes over for soda crackers and Coke. The smell of bacon frying makes her sick somethin' awful. But she's thrilled, Neal. And the kids are, too. They can't wait for the baby to come."

We chitchatted the subject to death, but the old man was ready. The first pause and he jumped in with both feet.

"I went and talked to the Captain, Neal." This sounded ominous. "He agrees with me that now that Angelesi's out and the whole thing is forgotten, you could get reinstated with no problem."

This was new territory. I had expected the usual reminiscing about the good ole days, his twenty-five years with the NOPD, the best years of his life, the lead-in to how I had ruined mine by messing with politicians like Angelesi and having to resign from the force before the Captain was forced to fire me.

He went on. "He wants you to come back, Neal."

Ma must have known this was coming because she had cleared out. I listened to the ironing board squeak in the next room as she ironed her doilies while I tried to think of something to say that wouldn't get him riled.

"I like the Captain, Dad. I'm glad he doesn't think too badly of me."

"Badly of you?" He smiled broadly. "He says you were a top-notch cop. Says it must run in the family." Well, cops, anyway, certainly run in this family. My grandfather was a cop and his sons, my father and his brother, were cops. Both of Ma's brothers were cops and my sister married a cop. "He wants to talk to you. Whadaya say we go down there this morning? Together."

What I would like about getting reinstated on the force would be getting reinstated as a son. I hated to end the first real friendliness the old man had shown me in over three years.

"Dad, I don't want to go back. I don't want to be reinstated."

He blew up. "I knew it. I knew it. Didn't I tell you, Mama?" he yelled. "You know what's the matter with you, Neal? You're just a goddamn stubborn jackass, that's what. Whadaya think? You gonna make a fortune bein' a private eye? You think you gonna get women? No, no not you. I could understand reasons like that. But you. You got these goddamn crazy ideas about changing the world or somethin'."

"If I wanted to change the world, I'd get reinstated."

I shouldn't have said that. He went from riled to furious.

The kids, who had been running up and down the stairs to the camelback of the house, became a major source of irritation.

"Get those goddamn kids off those stairs," he bellowed. "Where the hell is Maureen?" He ran off raving toward the front of the house, Ma right after him.

The back door opened and Michael swaggered in, gun in holster, nightstick dangling. He was just coming off night duty.

"What's going on?" he said jovially. "Is the family at war again? How you doin', Brother Neal? How's business? If things get rough, call the cops. You know the number." The Channel is teeming with good-natured tough guys like my brother-in-law.

"Just fine, Sarge, just fine on both counts."

"So you heard. I guess the old man told you." For some reason Michael thinks our family problems are hilarious.

"The first thing he said. Before good morning."

Michael laughed. "Yeah, he's proud as hell. Reminds him of the good ole days."

The good ole days. I thought I'd feel better down at the office.

2

The Luck of the Irish—
I Play Pool and Get a Case

I WAS GLAD TO GET AWAY from the familiar tree-less streets and the hard, exposing glare of the Channel. Without the blue uniform on I was a stranger and suspect. My own father didn't recognize me. Proud man that he is, why won't he understand that I can't go back to the NOPD? I took a lot of abuse when I suggested that Angelesi was responsible for Myra Ledet's murder. The old man was wrong saying I wanted to change the world. I had been in love with Myra since I had met her, and I knew from the beginning that she was sleeping with Angelesi, too. It drove me crazy sometimes, but he could pay her more.

So what if Angelesi has finally taken a fall? I would like to forget the whole thing, but I can't. And there's not a damn thing I can do about any of it.

The office looked good to me while I was over at the old man's, but when I got there and took a look at the spotted glass and my toothbrush sitting on a sink behind a folding screen, I knew I'd be better off at Curly's.

Curly's is a dive on the scruffiest block in the Central Business District, an eight-minute walk from my office in the Jesuit Fathers' building. The other advantage to Curly's is that it's open twenty-four hours a day, and although from

[5]

the outside it looks like it's boarded up, under the ragged
and sooty fight bills announcing Christian competition at St.
Mary's gym in the Channel there is always some shark on
the premises waiting to bleed five for his skills.

The regular shark at Curly's was Murphy Zeringue. I
couldn't remember when I hadn't known Murphy. We'd
gone through St. Alphonsus, then Redemptorist together,
skipping out at any chance from under the scrutiny of the
nuns so we could go over to Acy's and eat po' boys while we
watched the big guys play pool. From them we learned how
to handle a cue stick, and from then on Murphy's interests
had not developed much. During the day he was always
downtown at Curly's shaking down as many fives as possible
so he could head uptown to Grady's in the Channel and play
for higher stakes at night.

Murphy called over to me as I got a bottle of beer from
the bar. "Hey, Neal, you in for a game of cutthroat?"

"Sure, Murph."

I watched while Murphy and a guy I'd never seen before
finished up a lukewarm bout of eight ball. The guy was big
though his muscles had gone to flab. There was something
peculiar about his looks. His brown hair was too short for his
big face and tiny, half-inch bangs edged his forehead. He
looked like a forty-year-old Boy Scout recruit, but he
smelled of bourbon. In that state he was no match for the
Murph, which meant that one of us had an easy five coming.
The idea of leaning over a cue stick for the rest of the day
became more appealing.

Murphy's laugh cut into the sound of clicking balls and a
five disappeared into his pocket. He stood there looking
both pleased and sorry he'd won, that laugh a demoralizing
one when the heat was on and you weren't. His buddy, with
a face as smooth and lifeless as the piece of dull metal shad-
ing the bulb over the pool table, seemed to be taking it all as
a matter of course, so we racked up, eliminating small talk

like introductions. The fellow probably wouldn't be around long enough for me to remember his name anyway. He stuck through two more games, though, before he got agitated and called it quits, by which time Murph and I were each five ahead. He muttered obscenities when he paid off the last time. I was glad to see him go.

"Who's the Boy Scout?" I asked Murphy.

Murphy liked that one. "Good ID, Neal. Wrong jerk. He's a real screwball, but an easy five."

Murphy and I set ourselves up with plenty of beer and settled into the real cutthroat stuff. Playing with Murphy is always cutthroat, whether or not that's the game, since he won't play for low stakes with anyone he knows well. It was understood we raised to twenty. But I felt hot. Before I knew it the day was passing the way a day ought to pass and a certain twenty-dollar bill kept passing, too. After a few games Murphy stopped laughing—which meant he had something important on his mind. As he racked the triangle of balls into line for the third time and still didn't find the right spot, he said, "Say, Neal, what say we put some *real* action into this game." He looked up from the triangle. "Fifty." A flash of smile replaced his stony gaze.

"You're on, Murph."

He laughed his peculiar laugh, expecting it to have its usual effect. But I had played pool with him enough times to know I had the edge, since he had raised the stakes on his round to win and had changed the game to business.

He found the right spot with no trouble and came around the table to break, hitching his pants up on his thin frame.

It was a beaut. Two solids sunk just as neat as could be on opposite sides of the table. If I hadn't known better I'd have whistled in admiration. The only shot he had was a long and difficult cut to the right pocket at the other end, but if he made it he would be set up to clean me. He lengthened his already long face by moving his jaw down. His eyes settled on the cue ball and he poked it nice and easy. It traveled to a perfect slice but it had been just a shade too soft. The ball went right to the edge and stopped.

"Holy shit," he whispered. This was as much rage as Murphy ever displayed and it was always quickly replaced by that laugh. He couldn't shake me now, though. It wasn't the prettiest setup I'd ever had, but I felt more than up to tackling it. I leaned into the cue stick and leveraged Murphy's ruin.

The first one was easy, the second one harder. The third raised perspiration on my upper lip. I was beading down on the arrangement so hard I didn't hear the footsteps behind me or feel the vibration they set off in the loose floorboards.

"Hello, Neal." There was only one owner for that voice. The perfect courtroom voice.

"Hello, Maurice," I said without looking up. I knew exactly how he would be standing, weight evenly centered on his heels, his arms hanging purposefully at his side, one clutching a black satchel, not a briefcase, a satchel. Hell, a schoolbag. And he would be dressed the same way he had dressed all the years I had known him, probably since he was five. The three-piece black Western-cut suit, the white shirt, the black tie, the exact measure of gold watch chain showing, his black cowboy boots symmetrically scuffed. His alert, intelligent eyes would be staring out of his boyish face from behind slightly lopsided glasses, not missing a thing.

Maurice and I had met while I was still a fledgling patrolman and he was a law student. We were from different sides of the track and as opposite as the parts of town we came from. The son of a wealthy lawyer, he grew up in the Garden District, although his family was considered *nouveau riche* by the people whose families had inhabited the area for generations. The Garden District is directly across Magazine Street from the Irish Channel, their boundaries making them appear to be mirror images of each other. There the

similarity ends. The money, the mansions, and the gentility
are in the cool and shady Garden District. In the Channel,
the shotguns and doubles are separated by alleyways and
the people are tough. A lot of the city's cops come from the
Channel, which should give you some idea about the place.
Its big claim to fame is that John L. Sullivan trained for his
fight with Jim Corbett here, but that isn't actually true. The
confusion is a result, no doubt, of Sullivan's having been an
Irishman. Something about the way Maurice and I grew up,
though, must have given our personalities similar boundaries and we became friends immediately. It had never occurred to me to be anything but a cop and it had never
occurred to Maurice to be anything but a lawyer. By the
time he was thirty he'd been to the Supreme Court twice
and by the time he was thirty-five he was considered the
best hot-shot lawyer in town. By the time I was thirty-five, I
was starting over, my career as a hot-shot cop finished. It
was Maurice who finally convinced me I'd never get anything on Angelesi. He also told me I shouldn't waste my
years of training and experience and gave me my first case.

I took low aim at the cue ball, hit, and pulled back fast. It
did its work precisely and came back to the spot I wanted.

"Nice," said Maurice, drowning out Murphy's laugh with
his highest compliment.

The next shots were a piece of cake so I indulged in some
conversation.

"Glad you dropped by, Maurice."

"I am not 'dropping by.' I was looking for you." He was
emphasizing urgency, not making a judgment on how I
keep my office hours.

"How'd you find me?"

"I considered hiring the Pinkertons, but then I remembered," he paused, "this place." Maurice is not very fond of
being anywhere other than a courtroom or a law office.

"Just keeping the concentration sharp with a little luncheon relaxation." I glanced up to see one of his eyebrows making its way down from a considerable height of forehead.

"I've got an interesting one if you're available." There was no double meaning attached.

"I don't exactly have an abundance of time, Maurice," I said, sizing up the eight ball. Murphy was beginning to show signs of strain.

"That's too bad. A client of mine is having some trouble, but I'm not ready yet to begin proceedings. I advised him that it should be investigated first." His enunciation was concise. If the most respected and feared lawyer in the city thought the matter wasn't ready yet for his talents, then it was bound to be interesting indeed.

"Anyone I know?" I asked. Murphy quit looking like a beaten dog.

"I'm sure," he started loudly. Then he lowered his voice, which is hard for Maurice to do. "I'm sure you've heard of him." He stopped to let me chew on that a while.

I called my pocket.

"I was hoping you'd see him in my office this afternoon."

"No doubt you advised him I'd be there." The eight ball traversed the length of the table and came right back to thud in the pocket. I turned to face Maurice. "Who is he?"

Maurice clenched his teeth slightly to keep the sound in. "Carter Fleming. And yes I told him you'd be there at two o'clock." He cleared his throat loudly. "Hell, Neal, half the police force is on overtime parking detail for lack of anything better to do. Business can't be that good."

"Make it two-thirty." Maurice knows that I'm a man of principle.

"Good." He turned and strode out of the bar.

Carter Fleming, huh? The *Times-Picayune* society editor had dubbed him a leading citizen, but in spite of that endorsement, he really was one—and from an old family that still had its money. But while other uptown socialites were turning their bank presidents into carnival kings, Carter Fleming was out buying up their banks.

Murphy was busy picking his ear up from my side of the table, but if I know how to read a face, he hadn't picked up as much information as he would have liked.

"Well, Murph, it looks like we'll have to pick this up some other time."

"Sure, Neal, at Grady's," he said and laughed. One hand dove into a pocket, but it wasn't coming out again—not yet. "Hot-shot client, huh?"

I pulled at an earlobe. "I'll get the games, Murph."

One thing I like about Murphy is he's quick on the pick-up.

"Great, Neal." He pulled out five crumpled tens and made a great show of smoothing them out on the edge of the table. "Next time we play for fifty right off, huh?"

"You're on, Murph."

The guarantee of high stakes gilded Murphy's laugh as he handed over my winnings. He had gotten exactly what he wanted after all.

3

One for the Books

I HAD BEEN SO GEARED UP to spend the day playing pool that I was sorry to leave Curly's. I was probably sorrier to leave the air conditioning, but from the way Murphy asked two marks seated at the bar if they wanted to play cutthroat, the temperature in the joint would soon be equal to the stakes. It wouldn't be like Murphy to let any more money slip through his fingers that day.

I had just enough time to have a quick lunch at the sandwich shop on the first floor of the good Fathers' building before heading over to Maurice's law office. The lunch rush was just about over, which left Leone a lot of time to banter me from behind the counter as she fixed a sandwich. I tuned her out and reviewed what I knew of Carter Fleming. There were a few different factions of Flemings now. The money was oil money and Carter Fleming had most of it and was the best known of the lot. He was constantly written up in the society section of the paper for some flamboyance or another. A patron of the arts who collected rare paintings and also bought the works of promising young artists from New Orleans and elsewhere, he had spread a little of the right kind of PR around, made names for some of the young promisings, and raised the value of his collection.

There was also a Mrs. Fleming whose charitable works and city beautification plans were often in the news. My memory failed me about the same time my sandwich arrived.

By the time I was ready to go to the garage and get my car it was well after two o'clock. The afternoon heat settled on my face as I stepped out of the sandwich shop. Gabe, the garage attendant, was persistently and to no avail mopping his sweaty black brow. We exchanged a few complaints and I took off.

The few minutes' drive over to Tulane Avenue took twice the time with the traffic meandering through the business district, but I managed to arrive with a couple of minutes to spare. Maurice's office was a small shotgun double that had been converted into law offices. His secretary, Pinkie, was, as usual in lax moments, sitting behind the desk preening her unrealistically long rosy nails. I had often wondered how she could type so well with them. I asked her.

She flashed me a big smile and said, "Easy," whipped a piece of paper into the machine, set it whirring, and within a split second had typed a single line. She handed it to me, cupped her chin in her hand, and looked at me demurely from behind thick lashes every bit as long as her nails. The line read: "Five o'clock is closer than you think. What's up?"

I gave her a long once-over. Her small, flawless face, made up in an attempt to look older, was framed by her short wispy hair. She looked pretty in the soft light thrown by the desk lamp.

"Things that a sweet young thing like yourself shouldn't know about," I answered.

"I'm not exactly a kid, you know," she said haughtily, and got busy trying to ignore me.

"No, you're not exactly a kid," I conceded.

With a cool glance she informed me that Fleming was already with Maurice. I stroked her smooth cheek with a finger and moved on down the hall to Maurice's office, knocked once, and opened the door.

Maurice was sitting behind his big mahogany desk. Fleming had drawn up a chair and sat hunched over the desk in Maurice's direction. He turned sharply and rose as I walked in. He was a big man with dark abundant hair and a smooth unlined face. He looked strong, but his stomach indicated that he lived the good life. His big handsome squarish face broke into a wide grin showing off big squarish white teeth. He stepped forward and extended his hand. I took it and got a hard politician's crush.

"Right on time," he drawled slightly in a loud, presumptuous voice. "I like that and I like what Maurice has been telling me about you, Rafferty. He says you're the best in the business." The grin got even wider.

Already I didn't like his attitude, but I remained cordial.

Maurice rose. "No need for you gentlemen to waste time. As I've explained, I'm not ready to begin proceedings and until such time, I'm sure my counseling won't be necessary. Since I am due at the district attorney's office, I'll leave you to discuss the matter privately." As Maurice stalked toward the door, the heels of his cowboy boots digging into the carpet, Fleming thanked him profusely. I sat down and lit a cigarette.

He turned back to me before Maurice had the door closed behind him. "Now," he said with a glance at his watch, "Let's get down to business." His voice was agitated and he dropped most of the drawl. "I've already wasted enough time and time is money."

I watched the ceiling and blew smoke at it. He cleared his throat noisily as my eyes drifted back to his.

"One week ago last Thursday I acquired at auction a set of expensive, rare editions of William Blake, the English poet, you know." He looked at me expectantly.

"Oh, yeah. The poet."

He stared at me a second. "There are eight books in the set, including the *Illustrations on the Book of Job* which is bound in Moroccan leather. The others are in calf. The bindings on a couple are a little loose and I wanted all of them inspected carefully and put in top shape. That would increase their value. So I had them shipped directly to Stanley Garber's shop on Royal Street and informed him they were coming. He does excellent work," he added parenthetically. "After I described the shape they were in, he said that the work shouldn't take more than a week at most. Toward the end of last week I called him, since I hadn't heard anything and I wanted to find out how much longer the work would take, but there was no answer at the shop. I found that strange so I called his house. His wife told me that he had gone out of town and she didn't know when he'd be back. I asked her if the books were ready, but she didn't know that either and told me she'd have him call as soon as he got back. Well, now, I didn't like the idea of nearly ninety thousand dollar's worth of books sitting in a closed-up shop like that. They're insured, of course, but I wanted to know where he went and when he was coming back. She wouldn't tell me anything. I've called the shop and the house several times since then. She tells me every time that she still hasn't heard from him. In my opinion, she doesn't know where he is. I think he's disappeared, and for his sake, those books better not have disappeared with him. I want those books found and if that means finding him first, then do it. That's the job, and the important things for you to remember are expediency and the safety of the books." He reached into his inner coat pocket and extracted a piece of paper folded lengthwise. "This is a detailed description of the books."

All the pertinent information had been typed up for me. He was efficient alright, like a man who expects to get exactly what he wants and usually gets it fast. I glanced at the paper, folded it again, and put it on the edge of the desk.

"Any questions?" he asked, and began to make motions of leaving.

"Plenty. Let's start with why you haven't gone to the police with this."

He glared at me. "What's the matter? Don't you want the job?"

"Not unless I know all the details."

He looked annoyed. "Look. I've known Garber for a long time and I've never had any reason not to trust him. I admit that it looks bad for him right now, but if he's got the right answers then I wouldn't want to embarrass him unnecessarily by bringing the police in prematurely. But if he doesn't have the right answers, I'll lean on him so hard he'll wish he was dead. Don't get me wrong—I'm not an unreasonable man. I try not to assume the worst."

He sat back. It occurred to me that Stanley Garber's embarrassment wasn't his chief concern, although he probably had convinced himself that it was.

"And the last time you spoke to him was to tell him the books were on the way?"

"No. He called me a week ago, last Monday, early in the morning. The books were due in that day. I'd had Barrow's, the auction house in New York, send them by UPS, but Garber said they hadn't arrived yet."

I raised my eyebrows. "He called you just to say they hadn't arrived?"

He made a gesture of impatience. "He called to find out if I was interested in selling them. Something about he might have a prospective buyer."

"That's a pretty important point to neglect."

His intertwined fingers lay in his lap. "Well, I didn't want it to look any worse for him than it already does." Such magnanimous benevolence. He was too proud to admit that it had simply slipped his mind.

"Did he say who this prospective buyer was or how anyone knew you had the books?"

His eyes darted up at me. "I didn't ask him who it was. I told him I wasn't interested in selling. And anyone who read last Sunday's paper would know I had the books. There was an article about them. You see, I'm going to loan them to the museum for a couple of weeks. They're supposed to go on exhibition this weekend. That's one reason I was anxious about how much time the work would involve." He leaned forward. "Frankly, Rafferty, it's possible that Garber sold the books out from under me to this prospective buyer. I hate to say it, but that's what I think. I think that's a good place for you to start."

"I thought you weren't going to assume the worst."

"Well, what's your explanation?"

"I don't have one yet, but it would be pretty stupid for him to do something like that. It would be too easy to trace the books' arrival and acceptance at the store."

"Well, whatever, I want those books recovered. *Someone's* got my ninety thousand dollars in his possession at this minute!" He took another peek at his watch.

As long as he was back on the subject of money, I brought up my fee. He gave me a thousand dollar retainer and told me his generosity above my set fee was contingent on a speedy recovery. His speech annoyed me, but I didn't squawk. I figured I would just have to chalk it up to his business habits.

And that was it. I didn't like the man or his methods, but I put the typed description in my pocket and told him I'd be in touch with him. We walked out together. As I passed Pinkie's desk, I gave her an exaggerated wink. She gave me a secret look that no doubt was supposed to mean something, but it was lost on me.

4

The Question of Class

WOMEN. Now why would the old man suppose that wanting to get women is an adequate reason for becoming a private cop? Surely he knows that to a woman the job is no more an attractive way of life than that of an ordinary cop. It has something to do with his fixation that women of all breeds fall like trees for us tough Channel types, although I'm not sure how he ties that in with being a cop. I, of course, a third-generation Irish American, know better. I know, for example, that the women on the other side of Magazine Street don't think we're tough, just low class. Yet, somehow, an isolated example will bear him out. The old man loves to be right and he thinks he usually is. Maybe it's because when he's wrong, it generally has to do with something I don't want him to know about. Anyway, when Catherine Garber fell for me, I was glad to give him full credit for being right. But I'm getting way ahead of the course things took.

Stanley Garber's house was located in Lake Vista on Mockingbird Lane. Here the houses really do face a lane and the only accessibility by car is through alleys flanking the backs of the residences. I parked on the boulevard in front of the stone walkway leading through tall shade trees and walked to the house. Everything was abnormally quiet. It was like walking through a sparse forest, a well-kept sparse forest, and I found myself tiptoeing through the area avoiding the twigs that lay on the ground.

The Garber place was a white brick house considered modern in the fifties. The curtains were drawn close, and like the rest of the setting it was in, the house had an unreal and uninhabited air about it like the suburbs on a Hollywood stage set. It didn't seem likely that anyone would come in answer to the bell, but the door opened just enough to show a frail drab woman. Her stance and expression made her look older than she probably was. She stared at me with large limpid blue eyes that didn't fit in her small drab face.

"I'm looking for Stanley Garber."

She hesitated. "He's not here right now."

"Mrs. Garber?" She still just stared. "Do you mind if I wait? I have rather urgent business to discuss with him."

"He's not in town." She started to close the door. I held it open.

"Then I'd like to speak with you, Mrs. Garber. Perhaps you can help me." I said it as gently as I could. The woman looked ill. "My name is Neal Rafferty and I'm representing Carter Fleming."

"I have already told Mr. Fleming . . ."

"I know. He told me he had talked to you. Please, may I come in? I won't take much of your time."

She backed away from the door as I pushed it open and went in. I walked through a small foyer into a formal, austere living area. There were no lights on in the house and the windows were heavily draped. My eyes adjusted and the room became less dark but no less dreary. Mrs. Garber sat on the edge of a chair and twisted a handkerchief around her fingers. I sat on the sofa without being invited.

"Mrs. Garber, I believe Mr. Fleming told you about the books your husband was working on."

"I know about them. There's nothing more I can tell you. My husband doesn't discuss his business with me. Why are you here?" Her voice was clear and stern but a little cracked around the edges.

"I'm a private investigator." Her hands stopped working, and the expression on her face tightened so that her features got larger but not stronger. The effect was produced by the deepening of the lines in her battleship-gray complexion; they deepened close to the edges of the apertures and became dark ravines into which her mouth, nose, and eyes might slide and disappear.

"Mrs. Garber—" I hoped I was being tactful enough— "Mr. Fleming tells me that he has known your husband for a long time and that it is not like him to be late with a job. He said that normally Mr. Garber would have phoned him if there was going to be a delay. What it is, Mrs. Garber—he's concerned, and that's why he asked me to look into the matter."

Hard as this was for me, I thought I was doing splendidly, but the more I talked the more drawn and constricted her face got. I knew there was something desperately wrong and I felt a sincere desire to help, but I was afraid that my presence was too much for her. I was getting just scared enough that she might have some kind of seizure that I was about to make my apologies and leave when I heard the lock being turned in the front door. Mrs. Garber's head jerked toward the sound. The lights came on. I had thought Mrs. Garber looked bad in the semi-darkness of the room. In the light she looked like she'd spent a week in a cancer ward chain-smoking Picayune cigarettes.

"Mother, what is it?"

Mrs. Garber turned back to me and one hand clutched at her throat. The movement frightened me. I thought she was having an attack and I jumped up to go to her. Catherine had entered the room. The glance her pale, icy eyes tossed at me glinted like steel and froze me dead. She dropped a drug store package and helped her mother from the chair. They left the room and I heard a door close toward the back of the house. I picked up the package and began to pace the room.

Catherine was the first woman I had seen in over three years who I thought was as beautiful as Myra. Poor Myra. The truth of it is that Myra would have been way out of Catherine's class. So there was the question of class and there was the coldness I had felt coming from her; I thought Catherine was unapproachable. But that didn't keep me from looking. Her hair and skin were almost the same color, a bronzy tone, like she'd been burnished by the sun, though she was unmistakably not tanned. Her hair was pulled away from her face and the color glowed from her cheekbones. Those gray-blue eyes were like chunks of ice in a fire. Her presence was very strong; the house had come alive with her in it. When she left the room it became austere once again. I wanted her to come back so I could look some more. I paced, thinking morosely about the circumstances under which I had come to the house.

It was a while before she came back. When she did I realized she was rather tall. She gave me another cold look. I'd seen people look cold like that when they'd been hurt.

"I'm Catherine Garber. My mother tells me you're a private investigator. I'd like to know what you think you're doing here."

"My apologies, Miss Garber. I didn't know your mother was sick. I would have contacted you first, but I didn't know Garber had a daughter either."

"Fleming knows exactly how sick my mother is."

"Then he neglected to tell me."

She gave me an appraising look. I told her who I was and repeated much the same story that I had told her mother.

"So you think Carter Fleming is concerned about my father," she stated. "I think you've been duped, Mr. Rafferty."

"No, I don't think so. Fleming wants his books back. That may make his concern for your father secondary, but it still makes him concerned."

"Sounds as if you know your client fairly well." She sat in the same chair her mother had occupied and took a cigarette from a box on a small table next to it. I gave her a light and propped myself up against an antique desk standing beside the door to the room. She pulled at the cigarette and sat back, giving me another cool look of appraisal. I looked back. She tucked the long fingers holding the cigarette into the palm of her hand. Her arms drew in close to her slender but well-built body. I wished she would relax.

"So you know Fleming?" I asked.

She nodded slightly. "My father has known him for years."

"From the bookstore?"

"Yes, and before that. They went through school together. But they haven't had much to do with each other for about twenty years."

"What happened?"

"It had to do with a business deal that didn't work out, at least not for my father."

"It did for Fleming?"

"Everything works for Fleming."

"What kind of business deal?"

She flipped a hand indifferently. "Look, why don't you ask Fleming? After all, you're working for him." She said it like I had warts.

"I will ask him. But just because he's my client doesn't mean I take everything he says as the gospel. There are always two sides, and I'd like to hear Garber's."

"What's the matter, Mr. Rafferty, don't you trust your client?" She smiled at me.

I didn't answer that. "Would you tell me about the business deal?"

The smile vanished. "Sure," she said slowly, "I'll tell you. I'd like you to know what a bastard you're working for."

Well, whatever the motive, I wanted the story.

She stubbed out her cigarette. "About twenty years ago my father heard of a piece of property in Texas, good land for oil speculation. He wanted to buy it. He's not a man to take such long-range gambles and probably wouldn't have been interested if the formation hadn't been so good. But he couldn't get a bank loan, since he had already extended himself setting up the bookstore. He must have wanted it badly because he called Carter Fleming and asked him to make the loan personally. They had been friends in college, but they hadn't seen each other socially for some years—the Garber name doesn't rate a listing in the social register."

She paused. "So, my father called Fleming and asked for enough money to make the down payment and start drilling. Fleming wined and dined him through several business chats at his house and even went with him on a scouting trip to see the land and give his celebrated professional opinion. And he agreed that the probability of oil was high and that it was a first-rate deal. Only when the deal was just about to go through, he called my father and told him that he was having problems with some of his drilling in the Gulf and that it was going to cost him so much that he couldn't afford to make the loan. So my father lost out. He was disappointed, but he accepted it, until he found out that Fleming himself had bought the land. The sale had gone through the day he called with his bad news and apologies."

"Does Fleming know that your father found out?"

"I wouldn't think so. Not from my father, anyway. It's not my father's style to lower himself and have a hopeless confrontation with a man like Fleming." She was quietly enraged. "That was when Fleming started telling anyone who would listen what a great artist Stanley Garber is. Fleming isn't concerned about my father. He couldn't care less. He probably doesn't even care about his books, just what they're worth."

I nodded. I felt sympathetic and I hoped she could tell because she wasn't going to like the next question. "How long has your father been missing, Catherine?"

"Who says he's missing?" she snapped.

"My intuition. I can tell things aren't right here."

She tried to hold on to her anger, but she couldn't. With the belligerence gone, she had become vulnerable. Her mouth trembled. She was controlling herself, but just barely. I lit a cigarette and handed it to her. The eyes that turned toward me when she took it were wounded and frightened. I didn't want to crowd her just now so I went back to my post against the desk and waited.

When she spoke, she whispered. "Mother. What am I going to do? She's so sick and he's been gone for a week." I thought she would cry now, but with another effort her control seemed firm.

"Why haven't you gone to the police?"

She shook her head. "She won't. She says she's sure there's a good reason why he left. I disagree—he's never gone anywhere without telling us where he was going. She says we should wait."

The corner of the desk felt like it had grown into me. I moved to the center of the room. "Any ideas where he might be?" None. "Does he leave often? To buy books?"

"No. Most of his buying is done by order forms."

"Do you help him with the business?"

"I used to until Mother got sick. Then he hired help."

I asked her who.

"A woman named Lucy McDermott. But she seems to have disappeared, too."

That bit of news excited me almost as much as looking at her, but she seemed unmoved. "Is that why your mother won't go to the police? Because she thinks your father and Lucy McDermott have gone off together?"

The anger flooded back, the tide carrying her to the center of the room to confront me. "How dare you . . ."

"Get off that," I interrupted. "If I'm going to help you, I have to try everything. And I don't believe in coincidences. Now what of it? Is that the reason? Is there even a possibility?"

She looked confused. I thought it was because I said I was going to help her, but the old man would have opted for women liking it when you get tough with them.

"No, no possibility. He wouldn't—he couldn't," she stammered. And then emphatically, "He wouldn't do that. I know him. And I know Lucy McDermott, too," she added in that mysterious undertone women get when they talk about other women.

I smiled. "Okay. What happened last Monday when he left?"

"Nothing happened. He went to the store."

"How do you know he went to the store?"

"He—of course he went to the store. He left early. He said he had work to do before the store opened."

"Did he mention the Fleming books to you, that he was expecting them?"

"Yes. He was very excited about them, that he was going to handle them. He loves old books."

"Enough to take them?"

Her face froze unnaturally. She shifted the weight of her body as if she were about to grab me and throw me out. Then she was still. "That's what Fleming thinks, isn't it?"

"It's crossed his mind."

"It would," she said bitterly. "My father would never steal anything."

"I want to take a look at the store." She didn't look at me or say anything. "Do you have a key?"

Without a word, she left the room. I turned to the desk.

There was a single picture of a younger Catherine which hadn't captured her extreme vividness and there was a picture of the three Garbers together. Mrs. Garber looked a lot better in it, but there seemed to be an underlying sadness. Maybe it was just because she wasn't smiling. Stanley Garber was smiling broadly, and while his portly looks were nothing more than mediocre, he looked like a pleasant sort of person, if that means anything.

A few minutes later Catherine returned and handed me a key.

"Have you been to the store since Monday?" I asked. She shook her head and said something about not wanting to leave her mother and having called there and at Lucy McDermott's apartment several times. I asked her if her mother was okay.

"She seems to be resting well enough," she said. I opened the door and started to leave. She stuck a hand out to touch my arm but pulled back quickly. It looked as if something was bothering her and our eyes were locked as I waited expectantly for her to say something. I waited long enough to know that something unusual had happened to me. Leaning forward, I kissed her lightly on the mouth. She didn't return it; she didn't look affronted; she didn't look surprised. She was almost as tall as I am.

5

A Different Kind of Luck

BY THE TIME I LEFT the Garber house there were other things on my mind besides Fleming's books. Maybe my motives weren't the purest, but I wanted to find Stanley Garber. It just so happened that was the best way to find the books. Catherine's anger at Fleming and her defense of her father had left an impression on me, to say the least. But it was her mother's refusal to take action that seemed most significant; I couldn't get the idea unstuck from my brain that she was afraid Garber had gone off with Lucy McDermott.

I wasted no time getting down to the French Quarter. Garber's store was in the seven hundred block of Royal Street amidst antique shops and boutiques which line both sides of the street. The front window of the store had Garber's Rare and Used Books written on it in gold leaf. Books whose pages looked so old and yellow that they would shatter if you tried to turn them were opened and displayed on small easels. Some manuscripts were strewn on the floor of the window, giving the effect of arranged asymmetry.

I opened the door with the key Catherine had given me, and immediately my senses were bombarded. The air was ice cold from an air conditioner that roared at me in the quiet of the room, and in the icy air there was a sickening odor. Faint but unmistakable. I found the light switch. There was a long counter to the back of the room. I looked behind it and found a couple of stacks of books. The rest of the room seemed okay, books on shelves to the ceiling, a bin of art prints. There was a door on the left side of the room. I went through it. Again, cold air, another roaring air conditioner. The light from the other room was enough that I could see that I had found Garber alright. Dead. The smell was bad so I covered my mouth and nose with a handkerchief and tried not to breathe too deeply.

Garber had been shot in the chest. His coat had been buttoned to hide most of the bloodstained shirt. It was a peculiar touch. His arms dangled loosely at his sides and his head hung over the back of the chair in an abnormal way. I looked to see what had kept him from falling. His legs were spread and the knees were braced on the side drawers of the desk. That and the arm rests had kept him in the chair. I looked at his face. Death had changed it considerably. He was the same man whose picture was on the desk, but I could no longer tell if he had been a pleasant sort. He was almost completely bald; the fringe around his head was gray. He was a big man and heavier than he was in the picture. He still had on his horn-rimmed glasses, but he was wearing them on his mouth. That didn't fit with the buttoned coat. I turned on the desk lamp to have a look around before I called the police. It would have to be quick; I couldn't take the stench much longer. Books lay everywhere, some on shelves and a lot more stacked on the floor. There was a large work table at the side of the room by a window where books were being bound and repaired. I checked them quickly to see if the William Blake volumes were there. Then I checked the rest of the room. It went fast. The leather-bound books were arranged mostly in groups, some behind glass. Somehow it had been easy enough to guess that Fleming's books wouldn't be there. I went back to the desk. There were more books on it, but not Fleming's. Under one stack near the telephone I saw part of a notepad. I pulled it all the way out. Two names were written on it, Fleming and Robert André. Both names had been traced over as if Garber had been on the phone when he had written them and had continued to doodle while he talked. I slipped the pad into my coat pocket.

It was time to leave—I was getting sick to my stomach. I went back to the first room, closing the door behind me but now that it had been opened, I couldn't get away from the smell. I didn't expect to find them in here either, but I checked the room for the books. As I went over the shelves, I noticed that a section of shelves behind the counter to the right was out of alignment. I pushed on it. The shelves had been built right over a door that opened into a long narrow room running parallel with the front room. I pulled the string on the bare bulb hanging in the center. More shelves, but these were filled with office supplies, order forms, catalogs, and ledgers. I pulled out the accounts payable books. Lucy McDermott's name and a Madison Street address were listed. She was certainly being paid well, three hundred dollars every Saturday for nearly a year. I put the book back and went over to the file cabinets, but there was nothing of interest, just copies of orders, brochures, and invoices. There was a toilet and sink at the end of the room. I turned the light off and closed the door securely. Shut tightly you couldn't tell there was a door there unless you happened to spot the knob in the conglomeration of books.

I closed the front door to Garber's and locked it. Garber's store was on the corner. On the other side a bricked carriageway that led to an open courtyard separated the bookstore from Royal Theatrical Supplies. The closed sign had already been hung in the door, but some lights were on and I could see a woman moving around, hanging costumes on a rack and putting things in order. I knocked. She came to the door and gave me an engaging smile while she jiggled the closed sign up and down.

I gestured at the bookstore. "Could you tell me when you last saw Stanley Garber?" I asked loudly.

She looked at me intensely through the glass and then unlocked the door. She was about forty and attractive, in a stagey way, her large features heavily made-up, her short hair dyed jet black. She wore a deeply fringed black shawl embroidered with bright colors.

"I was wondering when someone would finally come." Her low, silky voice undulated like the fringe on the shawl. "I don't think anyone has been over there for a week."

"You're not sure?"

She pointed at the air conditioner protruding from high up the brick wall of the carriageway. "He usually turns the air conditioner off at night, and I haven't seen any lights."

"When last week did you see him?"

"Last Monday morning. He was standing in the doorway talking to a young man when I opened up."

"Do you know who that was? Could you tell me what he looked like?"

"No. He had his back to me."

"How do you know he was young?"

She smiled at me indulgently. "I could tell by his stance, the way he held himself. I notice things like that."

I looked past her, into the shop, at the costumes and Styrofoam heads with wigs on them. My eyes came back to her jet black hair. I hadn't realized she was wearing a wig. "Of course," I said. "Could you tell me anything else you noticed about him?"

"Sure. He was tall, taller than Garber. He had on blue jeans and a T-shirt. His hair was long, shapeless, brownish. He was holding a box. Would you mind coming inside? I'd rather not air condition the street."

Everyone is sensitive about their air conditioning in the dead heat of August.

As I stepped inside she flexed her nose at the smell that was still clinging to me and gave me a peculiar look. I forged ahead quickly.

"What about the lady who works for Garber, have you seen her?"

She laughed a slithery laugh. "The kind of hours Lucy keeps, she's got to be balling him for her salary."

My eyebrows shot up in surprise.

"Oh, come on," she said, "surely in this day and age you're not shocked." The way she said it, I felt foolish for letting her see my amazement even if she had misinterpreted it. "Who are you anyway? Have I been indiscreet?"

Somehow this interview was going awry. Maybe it was because I was still shaken from seeing Garber's dead body. In my line of work, the last thing I wanted was for her to think she'd been indiscreet, but she hadn't asked like she was very worried. I thought instead she had sensed my embarrassment at letting my face be read so easily and was amused. Well, it was her turn in the trenches now. I am, after all, a tough guy from the Channel.

I hit her with it. "I've just been next door and Stanley Garber is dead. Murdered."

Her face registered nothing. A big zero. A cold fish. It irked me. I found the phone by myself and called the police. She had gone beyond the rack of costumes, to the far end of the room where there were two dressing tables, over them mirrors bordered by light bulbs. She was sitting on a stool in front of one of them, the shawl pulled close around her like she was very cold. She stared at the floor. I sat on the other stool, warming up for some third degree. She lifted her head and I could see I had called it wrong. The emotion stood out on her face. I felt like a jerk.

Her name was Eva Adams. She told me that as she'd

walked up that Monday morning, Garber was speaking in low, rapid tones to the young man, striking the box he was holding for emphasis. She had heard his fingers thump the box but could not hear what he said. As she came into the carriageway, he had nodded to her and pulled the guy inside. This was just before ten o'clock. After that she had heard and seen nothing.

Lucy, she said, kept very irregular hours, so that Eva wasn't sure whether she'd been in the shop or not during the past week. That, the way she dressed, and her possessiveness when she talked about Garber or the bookstore had led Eva to assume that they were having a sexual relationship. She said she did not speak to either of them very often and did not know them very well.

The NOPD was on the scene quickly. I was unlocking the door for the lab boys when Roderick Rankin lumbered up.

"I rushed right over when I heard you'd called in a homicide, Neal." He went past me unhurriedly, straight back to Garber's office, elephantine in his light gray summer suit.

I waited in the carriageway and cursed my luck and a damn town where you can't go anywhere without running into someone you know. If I'd had to find Garber's body, why couldn't I have done it on his day off?

Rankin is no ordinary cop to me. He just happens to be one of the old man's best friends. The old man had been on the force a few years when he and Rankin were assigned to the same car. From then on he was Rankin's mentor, leading the way in rank until they ended up on Homicide together. Rankin had been in on many of our family discussions, and he had notably contributed to the idea that I was ruining my life trying to get the dope on Angelesi. He was the first to suggest that I resign from the police department before I was fired. I wondered if he was in on the old man's latest plan for my improvement.

He joined me in the carriageway. "What a way to start the week, huh, Neal?" His eyelids were heavy, dopey looking.

He gazed at me from underneath them.

"You said it, Uncle Roddy."

"You touch anything?"

"Uncle Roddy!"

He had a silent laugh, but you could tell he was amused because air rushed out of his nose and his jowls shook. "Just checking, just checking on you, Neal." He waited for me to say something, but I just stood there trying to look like I appreciated his sense of humor. "Who gave you the key?"

I told him. His bushy eyebrows drew together.

"She your client?"

"She isn't paying me, if that's what you mean."

"Why'd she give you the key, then?"

"She told me her father was missing and gave me the key."

"He isn't on the missing persons list."

I shrugged.

"So why'd she call you in?" he demanded.

"She did not call me in, Uncle Roddy."

His eyelids got so heavy I thought he was going to sleep. "Okay, Neal, let's have the background on this."

I took a deep breath. "Look, Uncle Roddy, I think I owe it to my client to talk to him first."

He blew air out of his nose and shook his jowls. "Neal, Neal." He put his fingertips on his chest. "This is me, your Uncle Roddy, Neal. You can tell me. Everything," he added. "Now, who is your client?"

I didn't like the way he was trying to manipulate me. "I don't have to tell you that, Uncle Roddy."

The slits he looked at me through got venomous. "That so? You forget this is murder. I can haul you in for withholding information."

"Well, I really would like to consult with my client first."

"Fine. We'll go consult with him together." I shook my head. "Don't be a stubborn jackass, Neal." Echoes of the old man. They must have talked already. Since they were calling me one, I decided to be a stubborn jackass.

"You know, Uncle Roddy, if there's one thing I learned from the New Orleans Police Department, it's that certain people in this city are untouchable. It has to do with politics and money. My client just happens to keep a lot of people's pockets heavy, which makes him a powerful man. He might not like it if you go barging in on him with no reason. He might get mad at you."

His eyes opened as wide as they ever had. "You get this straight, Neal. I don't like no two-bit detective using scare tactics wit' me. There ain't no one in this city who's above the law as far as I'm concerned."

"Yeah. Like Angelesi."

"He got his in the end."

"Not for my two bits he didn't."

"Being in love with a dead girl must not be very satisfying, if you get what I mean."

"I get what you mean," I said, tight-lipped. "I should have made an anonymous phone call."

He rocked back on his heels, pleased with the dig. "Maybe you should have if you weren't going to cooperate. What you gotta realize is, even if you are John's son, I gotta treat you like everybody else."

"That's all I ask, Uncle Roddy, just to be treated like everybody else. Forget you know me. Forget I'm John's son. And I'll forget you asked me to betray my client's confidence just because you're my old man's friend."

I got a nasty gaze through reptilian slits. "Go easy, Neal. Go real easy. I'll get your license if you're withholding evidence."

I forced myself to say that was fair enough.

He went over to Royal Theatrical Supplies. "Stay available," he said and pushed the door open. I hoped he would have a long and satisfying conversation with Eva. Her assumptions about Lucy McDermott's sex life with the dead man would keep his mind off me for a while.

6

Hands Off

THE STENCH of Garber's body had stayed with me. I needed to get rid of it so I headed in the direction of St. Charles Avenue to the Euclid Apartments which I now call home although for me home will always be the Irish Channel. Shortly after Myra's death I had left my parents' house for good. The situation with the old man had become intolerable. He kept saying there was no good reason for Angelesi to kill the likes of Myra.

I took time to shave and hurried back out to the lake. I didn't expect my bad news to make me an immediate favorite of Catherine's, but somehow the fact that I had kissed her made me the man to tell her.

I parked in the same place in front of the lane and started for the house. There were lights on in the houses and among the trees. Nighttime made the place look more real.

I knocked softly and hoped Catherine would answer. She did. She had on the same dress, a close-fitting cream-colored dress with short sleeves. The soft material made a tight circle around her upper arms. The flesh under the circle was full and firm and a rich golden color. She had let her hair down. It brushed her shoulders. I wished there was nothing else to do that night but decide if she looked better with it off her face or down.

The icy blue had melted away and left a gray mistiness about her eyes, creating a strange and shadowy look that was hard to read.

"Did you find Fleming's books?" she asked, and stepped aside to let me in. Her voice was tired and bland.

I took her arm and guided her into the living room. "No, I didn't, but that doesn't matter. I'd like to ask you a few more questions."

"Sure," she said with a brief gesture of indifference that neatly disengaged her arm.

"How long has your father known Lucy McDermott?"

The mist vanished. "Look. If you're going to start with that again, you can leave."

"Stop that," I said softly. "That's not what I meant at all. She's worked for your father about a year?"

She nodded.

"Do you know where she's from?"

She thought a moment. "Maybe Florida."

"Where in Florida?"

"I don't know," she said irritably. "I'm not even sure she's from Florida. All I know is she had an aunt there who died and she took care of everything. I can't even remember when it happened. March, April; sometime after the first of the year."

Maybe that was something and maybe it wasn't. I turned and walked across the room. "Did your father know her before he hired her?" I asked with my back to her.

There was a lot of silence. I turned to see her staring at me like she thought I'd lost my mind.

"Should he have? Is it written somewhere that you have to have a long-standing friendship with a woman before you employ her?"

I went back to where she stood and put my hand on her

arm. "No, Catherine. Of course not. Hey, are you always so angry?"

She moved away from me and sat down heavily on the sofa. "No. No, I'm not." Again, she drew her arms in close to her body, one folded across her middle, but she held up a hand like she wanted to keep me away from her. "It's just that you—you're making me angry. I don't even know why I'm talking to you—you work for Fleming." The hand gestured at me. "What is it about you? What is the point of all this?"

"I'm sorry, Catherine. I don't want to make you angry. I want to—look, just tell me—" I thought about Lucy's salary and Eva saying she didn't keep regular hours. "I'm puzzled, that's all. He was paying her three hundred dollars a week. He must have thought a lot of her."

She jumped up. "Damn you! You won't leave it alone, will you? You *want* to believe that he ran off with that woman. That makes it simple, doesn't it? I tell you, he didn't!" She was flushed, her fists clenched.

"I know, I know." I took both of her full, firm arms. She was taut against me. "I know he didn't, Catherine." And I told her how I knew. She just stared with the stare of a somnambulist, dreamy but trancelike. Then her eyes started to dilate. Very slowly the pupils enlarged until the gray-blue became almost all black. She was in shock, but there was an incredible depth in those eyes. The black was so deep that it was hard to tell if the light in the room was being reflected or if it had fallen in. I gripped her and moved her to the sofa. Her body was stiff and seemed to be trying to reject the movement. Once she was sitting, I rubbed her hands and then her face and tried her name out on her, but she was gone. I was getting worried. The only thing I could think of was a bottle of brandy I could see in the next room. I poured one, drank it and poured another, and brought it back to the sofa with me.

A few minutes later she startled me when she said, "My father did not run off with Lucy McDermott."

"I know," I managed, jolted. I picked up the glass of brandy. "Here, drink some of this." She took a sip and asked for a cigarette. I gave her one which she puffed once, put in an ashtray, and forgot about.

We sat for a while in silence. I finally had to say it. "Catherine, do you remember what I told you?"

She looked pained. "I can't cry," she said. I told her it was okay. She said she wished she could and wondered if everything would ever be alright again. I said it would. I stroked her hair and tried to give her some assurance. She closed her eyes and seemed to relax, but only briefly. Her eyes snapped open and she withdrew in panic.

"Mother." Her voice was hoarse. "How am I going to tell Mother?"

We talked it over and decided that it would be best if Mrs. Garber's doctor were present with a sedative. Catherine accepted my offer to call him and told me that his number was written on the back of the telephone book by the hall phone.

When I returned her grief was evident and she seemed anxious for me to go. I thought she would have her cry once she was alone. I told her to expect a visit from the cops and she said that she could handle it. She saw me out with hardly a good-bye.

7

A Liar Will Steal, a Thief Will Murder

To A COP ON THE BEAT, the French Quarter at night is like a lunatic asylum. The streets are filled with mad drivers who think they have found either the local dragstrip or the scenic route through town. The first type are too busy chattering to their cohorts to look where they are going and the second group use their side windows as windshields. The sounds are yelling horns, shrieking tires, and general clatter. Those few who are using the narrow streets to get somewhere experience serious frustration and the fright of a driving instructor who finds out his student is blind. The side streets are dark and safe only for junkies and pimps. Bourbon Street is an impasse of pedestrians who are either drunk rabble-rousers or sightseers or both. From Burgundy to Decatur there are panhandlers looking for a handout for their next high, for condoms, or for their religious organizations. The latter are the worst. They want your money and your soul.

The afternoons are not much better. The scum come out of their subterranean dwellings to crowd in doorways making deals and talking lingo. The tourist busses block traffic and the horse-drawn carriages leave sights and smells enough to jolt the sensibilities of a sewer worker. In the summer the streets get hot enough to fry an oyster.

But in the morning just after dawn has tipped the roof-tops with translucent color and the dampness smells like freshly ground parsley, there is no better place to be. Cool ruffles your eyelashes and your skin breathes the dew. The streets are empty but not forsaken. The pastel colors of the buildings emerge and wink in the sun. The quiet is backed by distant city rumblings making your isolation apparent. The early morning used to make my chest tight with a quiet, thoughtful kind of pleasure.

That night as I drove into the Quarter I got the same chest-tightening surge. It surprised me. I thought it meant I was finally losing my cop's view of everything and becoming an ordinary person. But then I realized that the presence of Catherine Garber in my consciousness was making me feel isolated from the rest of the world the same way that being the only one around to see dawn coming over those rooftops did.

The wooden door to Lucy McDermott's Madison Street apartment just off Decatur was locked. I started ringing all the doorbells until someone buzzed the lock open. A frizzy-haired, white-faced young man came stumbling out of his courtyard apartment. I told him I was looking for Lucy McDermott. He pointed up the stairs and went back inside. A whining guitar sound floated around the courtyard for a few seconds. I went up to the top floor and knocked on the door to Lucy's place. I got an answer from the floor below.

"Mister." I took it to be a throaty woman's voice. "You, up there." The voice had a coughing spasm.

I leaned over the banister. A slightly bent old lady craned up at me. I walked down to the landing she was standing on. She had on a dirty white blouse, washed-out red pedal pushers, and red rubber sandals that grabbed between the toes. Her dull gray hair was pulled into a ponytail that trailed thinly to the middle of her back. Her almost perfectly round head seemed to bob on its neck as her myopic eyes found my face. Her small pert nose was only a fraction above a turned-down mouth which the network of facial wrinkles emptied into.

"She's not up there anymore. Been gone over a week," she said and winked at me. "Are you one of her friends?" The eye winked again and she drew one side of her mouth down even further to control it.

"No, I don't know her."

"No. You're young enough to be one of her friends, but you don't look like the type." For some reason she left the "p" sound off the end of type and her mouth stayed open mid-word.

"When did she leave?" I asked, controlling my impulse to flick her mouth shut.

"I'll ask the questions, mister," she snapped with more energy than I had credited her with. One foot slid along the floor, moving her to the side and into better focus. She blinked. "You a cop?"

"Sort of," I replied, peeved at her astuteness.

"You mean you're a private eye?" I nodded. "You could have said so in the first place, mister. She in some kind of trouble?"

"Not that I know of. I'd like to ask her some questions. I could ask you some instead."

"And I could tell you a lot, if I wanted to. What else I got to do but snoop?" I couldn't tell if she was being sarcastic or not.

"I wouldn't want to push you into anything."

She thought about that for a moment while we stared each other down. "You got a cigarette?" she asked. I said I did and got invited in.

She led me into a front room that had too much furniture in it. There were chairs of every assortment and period lining the walls and little tables with broken legs and marred tops scattered among them. It was like a showroom in a Magazine Street "junque" shop. A rocker was pulled almost to the glass of an old-time box television set. Religious pictures ran in a row along the wall. Slung across the corner of one was a rosary. Over the middle one a crucifix leaned precariously into the room. On the opposite wall was a yellowed picture of a beautiful young woman. She saw me looking at it and flapped over to take it off the wall. She handed it to me.

"That's me—a long time ago. Longer than I care to admit." The comment was unemotional.

"A real knockout," I said and meant it.

"Yeah. Sit down so I can see you." She moved the rocker around to face me and wrapped wire-rimmed glasses around her ears. "I didn't have to wear a bit of makeup, not even rouge. She wears too much. Looks like an act for Ringling Brothers."

"Miss McDermott?"

"Who else? That's who you're here to talk about, ain't it? What about that cigarette, mister?"

I offered her the pack. She took one out and folded her legs under her. I lit us both and she closed her eyes, taking three puffs in succession as if she were smoking a peace pipe. A fit of coughing followed the third inhale. "I don't smoke too often," she muttered. "What's your name, mister?" I told her. "Okay, Rafferty, what is it you want to know?"

"Could you tell me what day it was Miss McDermott left?"

"Sunday. A week ago. In the afternoon."

"Do you know where she was going?"

"No. Miss McDermott and me weren't too sociable. Look, Rafferty, don't you want to know any of the good stuff?"

"Absolutely, Mrs. Parry."

"How do you know my name?" she demanded.

"It's on the mailbox downstairs."

"Oh. Right. Now, let me tell you about Lucy McDermott. She's no spring chicken anymore, though you couldn't tell by the way she acts. In the," she screwed up her eyes, "I guess year or so she's been up there, she's had all types and descriptions of men up there with her, but they're all younger than she is and they all look like losers. There's one that goes up there regularly—his name is Louie—and when he ain't around she has plenty of others. I usually don't see them more than once or twice. You should of seen some of them, Rafferty. One kid, and I mean a kid, had hair all the way down his back—as long as mine." She twisted an arm around to feel the point at which her ponytail hit. "He was skinny and dirty. He was disgusting, but I kind of felt sorry for him. You know? One day when I came home he was waiting for her out by the front door. I had seen him go up there with her before. I try to be neighborly, even when it ain't returned, so I asked him if he wanted to come inside and wait. He gets in here and sees all my pictures around and he starts talking religion with me. I don't trust no stranger that talks religion with me, Rafferty. I could look at him and tell he was a weirdo, but then he starts telling me all about his hocus-pocus religion, that Satan and God are one and the same in his religion. I told him I never heard of a religion like that and that the only true religion is the Catholic religion. I told him talk like that would get him damned to eternal hell. He said that if it wasn't so about God and Satan being the same, then why did God let people practice human sacrifice on Jesus? I took that crucifix there right off the wall and ran him down the stairs and clear out of the building with it."

I told her I was impressed and asked her about Louie before she could get going on religion again.

"Louie's her regular boyfriend. He's a big brute of a thing. Mean looking. When he's here they stay up all night drinking and fighting. He stays for a couple of days and then he's gone for a while. After he leaves I see a lot of liquor bottles in her garbage. I'm always glad when he leaves because then I can get some sleep. But I never complained about the noise. Not one time, Rafferty. So one night I was feeling kind of sad and lonely and I thought a drink might cheer me up. I didn't have any liquor here so I went upstairs and asked her if she would give me some. Just one drink. She outright lied and told me she didn't have any. I've put up with enough yelling and stomping around up there that her lying like that made me mad. I told her I'd appreciate it if she'd keep the noise down. So she tells me she'd appreciate it if I'd keep my nose out of her business. I told her if the noise didn't stop I was going to call the landlord. She told me she didn't care if I called the landlord. Well, I guess she didn't. She left the next day. You know what, Rafferty? I didn't mind all the noise half as much as I minded her lying to me. I can't stand that kind of dishonesty. If you'll lie, then you'll steal. If you'll steal, then you'll murder."

"Did Miss McDermott leave with Louie?"

"No, she left with a woman. And you know what else, Rafferty? I think she left on the sneak." I raised my eyebrows. "You know, without letting the landlord know. There hasn't been a soul up there at all since she left. Not anyone even to clean up."

Now there was a bit of information I could use. I asked her about the woman.

"She was here about half an hour before they left."

"Did you know her?"

"I don't know anyone who goes around with her."

"Let me phrase that a bit differently. Had you ever seen her before?"

"Never."

"What did the woman look like?"

"That I can't tell you."

"I thought you saw them leave together."

"I did, but she had on one of those wide-brimmed hats."

"Then how do you know you never saw her before?"

"Look, Rafferty," she said giving me a multiple wink, "I didn't even need my glasses to know that. I never saw *any* women visit up there. Only men."

"Could you tell if she was short or tall or old or young?"

"All I could tell through the curtain," she pointed at the sheer on the window, "was that she was on the thin side."

I reached over and patted her on the shoulder. "Thanks, Mrs. Parry. You've been a great help."

"I smell liquor on your breath," she said, her glasses glinting.

"That's strange. I just had an onion before I came up here."

"Funny, Rafferty. You got any more?"

I told her I didn't, but I'd bring her some if I came back.

"You do that, Rafferty. If I miss something because I don't have these on," she said fingering the wire on her glasses, "I still hear pretty good." Her nose was pretty good, too, if she could smell a brandy over an hour old.

She followed me out on the landing and watched me leave. I went back down to the courtyard and stayed there for a few minutes. I wanted to take a look around Lucy's apartment, but I didn't want Mrs. Parry to see me going back up there. She might think that was dishonest, or, worse, she might want to come with me. I started back up keeping close to the wall until I reached her doorway. I stopped for a minute to listen. I could hear water running. I ducked down and passed in front of the window and stopped again. The door didn't open. I moved toward the other side of the landing until I could just see in. She was standing at the sink. I hoped her peripheral vision wasn't too good and started up the stairs. I waited a moment in front of Lucy's door. I heard nothing.

I tried the door. It was locked. A thin strip of metal was peeling away from the side of the slatted window high on the opposite wall. I pulled it off and went to work on the lock.

Lucy hadn't bothered to clear the trash out of her apartment. Clothes were heaped in one corner and a few pairs of chewed shoes were scattered about. In the kitchen there were empty Jim Beam bottles, some pots and utensils. I opened the refrigerator. There was nothing in it but half a bottle of soda water. In the second room the bed had been stripped down to a stained mattress. There were more discards and empty bottles. I looked in the clothes closet. Coat hangers and a wad of crumpled newspaper were on the floor. I picked up the newspaper and looked through it. It was a few pages from the society section dated August 17, the day before Lucy had left. There was an article about a tea given by Mrs. Mathilde Fleming. It described who had been there and what they had worn. I wondered if it was a clue.

I went into the bathroom, which was right off the bedroom. On top of the toilet tank was a plastic brush with some reddish hairs tangled in it and a can of shaving cream. That was all. In the third small room behind the bedroom was an empty bookcase with an old Underwood on top of it.

I was making my way back to the front door poking around once more in case I had missed something when I heard the heavy tread on the stairs. It reached Lucy's door and then a pounding started that jarred the walls of the apartment so hard that the pots rattled around on the drainboard.

A man's voice called out, "Lucy, open up," in a demanding tenor. He kept banging. "Come on, Lucy," he whined, "it's me." He started kicking the door.

I opened up for him. He stared stupidly at me, swaying slightly. True to Mrs. Parry's description he was big, but his muscles had gone to flab. I looked at his brown hair that was too short for his big face and the tiny, half-inch bangs that edged his forehead. He was the Boy Scout I had played pool with at Curly's. Big boy, still stinking of bourbon, had been playing with more firewater and was not too steady on his feet.

"Where's Lucy?" he yelled and looked past me into the room. His lower lip stuck out in a snarling pout as he took in the abandoned apartment. He more or less stumbled inside and went to take a look at the bedroom. "What the hell is going on here?" he demanded, turning back to me.

"Looks like we both missed her," I said.

"Who are you?" He came over for a closer look. "Yeah, I thought so. You're that pip-squeak Zeringue's friend. That son of a bitch pickpocketed me and I don't plan to forget it."

"You better watch who you call a pickpocket."

"You watch, asshole. I'm gonna get him for it."

"Don't fool with Zeringue, pal."

He stepped closer, putting up a menacing fist. "What are you doing here, asshole?" I looked hard at him, feeling the anger rise into my throat. "Tell me where she is."

I shouldn't have, but I baited him. "I wouldn't tell you even if she wanted you to know."

"Why you son of a lousy . . ." he trailed off to concentrate on his big arm that was coming around in a mighty swing meant for my head. I ducked. He must have been too drunk to pull his punch because it kept going. It was forceful enough that it took him with it. He fell flat on the floor and his face hit with such a smack that it gave me sympathy pains. I heard soft flip-flops coming up the stairs. Mrs. Parry arrived securing her glasses to her face. She looked at the collapsed Boy Scout.

"Did you kill him, Rafferty?" she asked. He began to snore.

"Is that Louie?"

"That's him alright."

I took her by the arm. "Well, I think he's going to be here for a while." She resisted my effort to lead her away. "I checked, Mrs. Parry. All the bottles are empty." We went down to her landing. "Look," I told her, "that fellow's likely to be mad when he gets up. If he tries to give you any trouble, call the police."

"You don't have to worry about me." She was annoyed. "What I want to know, Rafferty, is why did you sneak back up here and break into that apartment?"

"I hate for you to put it quite like that, Mrs. Parry. Let's just say I suspected possible foul play up there."

"You know, I'm not so sure you're on the level, Rafferty."

I ran out of bribes when I gave her my last pack of cigarettes.

It was ten-thirty when I got to the car. By now Rankin would have shaken Catherine down and be hot on Fleming's trail. That meant Fleming would be calling my apartment and office looking for me. He would have to wait. I had one more stop to make to satisfy my curiosity.

8

Rafferty on Location

I STOPPED at an all-night drugstore on Canal Street to look up André's address. The usual array of Latin pimps was standing on the corner or leaning up against the building with their knees bent at forty-five-degree angles.

There were two Robert Andrés listed, one at 3201 Coliseum, a Garden District address, the other in Gentilly. I put my money on the first, and took Magazine Street uptown. To quiet the persistent rumblings of my stomach, I turned into the Channel on Third Street and grabbed a beer at Parasol's. And while it was still on my mind, I got a fifth of Jim Beam to keep in the car in case I visited Mrs. Parry again.

The 3200 block of Coliseum was shrouded with massive oak trees. Where I expected 3201 to be, a high ligustrum hedge obscured the house. Cat's paw had taken over the iron gate, making it hard to find in the dark. It gave a squeal of stress as I pushed it back.

The yard would have been a great location for an episode of Ramar of the Jungle. Grass was fast obliterating the brick walkway to the house, a large raised cottage. Even in the darkness I could see dark paint peeling away from the banis-

ters and railing around the portico. Long French windows
at the sides of the front door were shuttered but I could see
light trying to seep through on the right side. As I stepped
up to the door a board groaned at the nuisance of my late
visit. I pushed the yellowed ivory bell anyway.

I heard ice tinkling before he opened the door. He stood
with a drink and cigarette in one hand, eyeing me with an
amused expression. The deep purple smoking jacket he was
wearing tinged his white hair the same color. He took the
cigarette out of the hand holding the drink and caressed it
on the way to his lips. I opened my mouth to speak but he
beat me to it.

"My dear fellow," he said through a cloud of smoke in an
accent I could have hung a Yorkshire pudding on, "there
aren't many who would venture through my gardens at
night. You must be anxious to see me."

"Anxious and brave." I showed him my ID. "Neal Rafferty, investigator. Private."

"How very interesting. I can't imagine what you would
want to see me about." His eyes crinkled playfully. "Well,
maybe I do have one small idea. Does that alert your curiosity, Mr. Rafferty?"

"Not much. I figure you know why I'm here."

"Come now, Mr. Rafferty, you're taking all the fun out of
it. Why don't you come in? Perhaps I can convince you to
take a more sporting attitude." He turned and walked back
into the wide hallway separating the two sides of the house.

The exterior had about as much in common with the inte-
rior as the Desire project has with the Garden District.
Deep blue carpeting ran the length of the hall and the walls
were stark white. There was no furniture, only paintings
hung as if they were being shown in a gallery. Above each in
the high ceiling was a single spotlight. The effect was quite
impressive. The paintings were varied: Some were portraits
of rather singular faces done in muted pastels; others were
abstracts in vivid, running colors. There were a few still

lifes. I examined the portrait closest to me. The face was in movement, its lines contorted and flowing into the background as if it were looking out from a pool of running water. The amused expression identified it as André. Scrawled in large black letters in the lower right corner was the signature Lise.

"A tribute by a talented young woman, wouldn't you say? Please make yourself comfortable in my study. I'll be with you momentarily." He gestured at a half-opened door and took off to the rear of the house.

In the middle of the study a Tensor lamp lit up an overstuffed leather chair. The rest of the room was darkened by towering brown bookshelves. My eyes were adjusting to the change when I got the feeling I was being observed. I locked eyes with a giant frog sitting on top of a writing table under a shuttered window. His ruby eyes bulged in their sockets at me. All over the book-lined room, from every vantage point, on top of the shelves, the books, peering out from a potted palm, scattered on the floor, frogs glistened and winked. There must have been a hundred of them, all peering straight at me as if my entrance had alerted their danger signals. A little one perched on an ottoman even had his head dipped in my direction to get a better view. Under this scrutiny, I eased back in a Morris chair, also in the middle of the room, and turned on the floor lamp next to it. André had been reading. The book lay open on a side table next to the leather chair. There was a ring of water where his glass had been. I leaned over to see the title of the book. It was called *States of Consciousness*.

André came in carrying a bottle of Hennessey and two snifters. "I hope my friends have kept you amused."

"Don't they know it's rude to stare at people that way?"

He chuckled. "I don't suppose anyone's ever bothered to tell them." He poured the cognac and handed me one.

"Since you seem to know why I'm here, André, why don't you tell me about it."

He asked seriously, "About what?" but his amusement returned before he finished the question.

"About Garber."

"I know he's dead, but, then, I imagine you know that, too."

"Then maybe you know that your name was plastered all over his memo sheet. Have any idea why?" He lit a cigarette, looking at me over the flame. "Let me guess, André. These deductions are hard, but I think I've got it. You must be the mysterious 'prospective buyer,' the one interested in the Blake books."

"How clever of you."

"Yeah, I'm real ingenious. Why those particular books, André?"

"I'm a great admirer of William Blake's. I like books in general." He gazed fondly around the room. "I like owning them for the sake of owning them. That's actually a rather common obsession. You see, Rafferty, I'm not unsympathetic to your plight. I'm trying to help you with the more difficult deductions."

"Gee, thanks, André. That's real chipper of you. Why the Blake books? I ask again at the risk of being accused of senile repetition."

"Honestly, Rafferty, I'm not trying to be crafty. I repeat, at the same risk, I admire Blake. I admire all of the English poets of that period. My shelves contain collections of Wordsworth, Byron, Shelley, Keats, Landor. But they sadly lack any good collection of Blake. Do I make myself clear?"

"Did your collections of Wordsworth, Byron, Shelley, Keats, and whoever all cost ninety thousand dollars?"

He smiled and stuck his cigarette into the corner of it.

"Were you trying to ruffle Fleming with the offer?"

"No, no, Rafferty. You're off the track now. The offer was made without Fleming's knowledge of who was making it. The offer was made directly to Garber and with explicit instructions that he should not tell Fleming who was making it."

"Why the mystery?"

"Why not? I enjoy a good mystery. Anyway, if Fleming had been interested in selling, why should he care who was doing the buying as long as the price was right?"

"What made you think Fleming was interested in selling?"

"I didn't think he was."

"You're making more sense all the time, André. How did you know he had bought the books to begin with?"

"I'm not as provincial as I may appear to be, Rafferty. I read newspapers as well as books."

"Okay, André. Your point." I sighed. "Let's go back again. Why the offer if you didn't think Fleming was interested in selling?"

"Let's just say that ninety thousand dollars is a lot of money. Maybe I didn't want to part with it, so I felt safe offering to buy the books."

"Okay, I get it. We'll just skip that one."

We sat back smoking cigarettes, drinking brandy, eyeing each other. My head felt like someone had pumped a pound of helium into it.

I asked quietly, "Where are the books, André?"

His eyebrows moved toward his nose. "But, my dear fellow, don't tell me they're missing!"

"Don't act like you don't know, André. You seem to know about everything else."

"Mine is the knowledge of the general public, Rafferty. That interesting tidbit was not mentioned in the newscast. I suppose Fleming made sure it wasn't. A display of his inability to control everything would embarrass him."

"You know what interests me, André? How you knew to contact Garber about the books. That *he* had them the general public did not know." For an instant the mirth left his face, but just for an instant. If I'd blinked, I'd have missed it like you miss a postage-stamp town. I knew it was childish, but I was immensely pleased with myself.

"A friend gave me the information." I indicated my disbelief. "It's quite true," he said. "The same friend contacted Garber for me."

I paused for ominous effect and to think a second. I decided to give it a go. "Your long-haired friend was seen leaving Garber's shop with the books, André." It was a shot in the dark and I didn't think it had worked; not a hair on his head budged.

"Ah, my dear Mr. Rafferty, I have tried to be hospitable to you, and I have enjoyed your company until now. I don't mind your not believing me—most people are liars anyway—but now you are implying that my friend is a thief. Really, my frogs have better manners. At the expense of ending my favorite self-indulgences, drinking and talking, I feel I owe it to my friend to ask you to leave." He continued to smile at me, but his eyes had gotten stony. The gambit had hit a nerve just as surely as the long ash of the forgotten cigarette between his fingers was going to hit the carpet.

"I'm not known for having much tact when I don't get answers, André." I got up to leave, but on a whim went over to the writing table and patted the big frog on the head. It seemed to like the attention.

When we got to the door André said, "You're an intelligent young man, Rafferty. You'll get your answers without any help from me. It will be better that way." There was no trace of amusement, none of the witty cynicism.

I thanked him for the brandy and left.

9

Family Connections

I WAS DRIVING to Carter Fleming's Audubon Place address feeling foolish and not so smart. I had just played verbal chess with André and made the wrong moves—I felt sure he knew the location of the Blake books but my strategy had convinced him that I should find them without his help. Yet I liked him anyway.

I was stopped at a red light on St. Charles Avenue when the idea hit. If I was right some loose ends were suddenly going to start flying together. I laughed out loud. The light turned and the driver behind me blew his horn as if the two were on the same circuit. I passed Audubon Place and headed to an open pay phone at the intersection of Broadway and St. Charles.

I called Maurice.

"Hello." Alert. At three in the morning Maurice would sound alert. I'm not sure he ever sleeps.

"Hope I didn't interrupt an exciting dream—or anything like that . . ."

Maurice never gets my little jokes. "I heard the news about Garber," he said. "Were you in on that?"

Garber's dead face, the glasses over his mouth, his buttoned coat, loomed up in front of me. "Yeah. I found him."

"You weren't mentioned. I thought you were Fleming calling again. He's frantically looking for you and mad as hell."

"That must mean Uncle Roddy was there breathing all over him."

"Rankin pulled this one? My condolences, Neal."

"I may need more than that. He's mad as hell, too, and he'd love to relieve me of my license."

"What does he expect you to do for a living? Has he made any job offers lately?"

"Not exactly, but the old man wants me reinstated."

"Oh, boy. You better play this one close to the cuff."

"I'm too perverse. It gave me a thrill thinking about Fleming humbling the Lieutenant."

Maurice laughed. "It would have thrilled Fleming, too, except that he's so put out over the whole deal. He needs to be convinced you didn't betray his confidence. Were the books at the store?"

"No. There's some funny business going on about these books, but I may have come up with something. Do you know Robert André?"

"I know of him. He's supposed to be a little strange."

"Does he have a son?"

"Not that I know of. I've only heard of a daughter, an artist."

"Does Fleming have a son?"

"Yes, but Fleming doesn't like to talk about him. It's a real sore subject. You've heard the situation before: Father wants son to go to college and then come into the family business but son has other ideas and takes off. What's André got to do with all this?"

"He made an offer for the books. Where's Fleming's son now?"

"He did some traveling for a while at Fleming's expense. Fleming told him to go on and get it out of his system and when the money ran out to come back home and he'd send him to school. But it didn't work out that way. Carter the Third never made it back, but I don't know where he ended up. The money got spent and Fleming refuses to give out any more until number three conforms."

It was better than I'd hoped for. "Maurice, that's the best news so far today and there hasn't been much. Do you know of any link between André and Fleming's son?"

"No. Look, Neal, I'm glad that was such good news, but give out with the stuff."

"You know you can't stand speculation not based on hard facts, Maurice. I'll be talking to you."

I got back in the car and pointed it once again in the direction of Audubon Place. I pushed on the accelerator considerably harder than I had before I made the detour to the phone booth.

10

My Son, My Son

AUDUBON PLACE is a quiet, wide street divided by a grass-turfed median called a neutral ground by Orleanians. Azaleas and myrtle trees dot the ground, and in the spring and summer the area turns into a multicolored floral show. Some of the grandest houses in the city are majestically spread at decent distances from each other along the street, their lawns tended to and manicured in a landscaped perfection reminiscent of a Los Angeles cemetery.

Audubon Place is also exclusive. Guards are stationed at both ends to keep out the riffraff. Once when I was a kid I was busted by one of them for using the private street as a cut-through from Freret to St. Charles Avenue. He got me for no headlight on my bicycle and no ID. I didn't know that he really couldn't do anything to me, and even though I gave him a phony name and address, for the next few days I was terrified that the old man was going to find out anyway. He wouldn't have cared about the headlight or ID, but I would have been black and blue for traveling so far from home.

Once again I was asked for an ID as I pulled up to the medieval-looking stone guardhouse on the St. Charles side, but this time I got no trouble. Fleming, thorough as always

with never a moment to waste, must have told the guard to
let me through and then phone him that I was on the way.
The guard told me the Fleming house was the one with the
towers. It was easy enough to spot. I walked up marble steps
to a fantastical gabled mansion with three turrets.

I presumed that she was Mrs. Fleming. She had blue-
white skin and blonde hair that was as stiff and well-shaped
as a shrub. She looked very tense.

"Oh, Mr. Rafferty," she said in a drawl that under the
right circumstances could have oozed Southern charm and
hospitality, "thank goodness you're here. Carter is just beside himself."

Fleming came flying across the marble foyer that was as
big as my apartment. "Goddammit, Rafferty, where the hell
have you been? And what's the idea—bringing the police in
on my business? If I had wanted to handle it that way, I
would have called them myself. I want answers and I want
them goddamn fast."

I wouldn't have expected a big man to quiver quite like
that. There was nothing to do but work some pure Rafferty
logic on him.

"Mr. Fleming, when there's a case of murder, if I refused
to tell the cops who my client is, if I withheld information,
possibly suppressed evidence, what would you expect them
to do to me?"

"Haul you in and take your license." He started to go on
but I interrupted him.

"And what would you have done if that had happened?"

"Christ, Rafferty, I'd have had it fixed up in no time."

"Well, then, why in the world would you think I had told
them anything?"

He looked confused, but he was beginning to get it. He
was also considerably calmer. "You didn't?" he asked.

"No. What did you think, I walked into the nearest police
station and laid it on them?"

He didn't like my tone of voice. "So how did they find out?" he demanded.

"They have their ways. You could figure it out if you thought about it. What I want to know is what did you tell them?"

"I didn't tell them a goddamn thing."

I grinned. "I knew you wouldn't."

"So they don't know anything?" He was looking rather pleased.

"I told them I'd come clean after I talked to you. And I'll have to—we'll both have to."

"So you have talked to them?" There was a hint of an accusation in the way he said it.

"Sure I talked to them. I had to let them know Garber was dead. Since I found him."

He was actually sympathetic. "I didn't know that, Rafferty."

I shrugged. "You had no way of knowing."

"What do they think? What do you think? Who do they suspect?"

"They don't exactly confide in me, you know, but just assume they suspect everybody who had any involvement at all with him. If you ask me, the body's been locked up in that store a good week. They'll probably start there."

He must have thought I was going to get graphic about the body. He glanced nervously at his wife. She didn't appear to be in the least disturbed about the body. She was looking at us both in a most pleasant way, the tension gone. I guess she was relieved that Fleming wasn't storming around anymore. I could imagine that it wasn't much fun for her when he was out of sorts. I guess, too, that a week-old body just wouldn't have much significance in her happy, tea-filled life. I hoped it would keep on not having much significance to her.

Fleming patted her on the shoulder and told her that he

and I were going to talk things over. She took her cue and went to the back of the house.

Fleming and I sat in the Victorian parlor, me on an uncomfortable brocaded love seat, him in what looked like an equally uncomfortable matching high-backed chair. I was concentrating on gracefully keeping my hip pockets stable on the slippery material covering the narrow seat. Fleming picked at his thumbnail, his brow furrowed in concentration. He had just given a low whistle, not at his thumb, but at my stating that André had made the offer for the Blake books. We had finally gotten around to the books, and Fleming had been upset that they hadn't been at the store.

"Robert André? That old coot inherited all his money and has never done a thing in his life but pretend to write his memoirs for the last twenty years. He had to get rid of all his domestic help a few years ago and that house is going to pot. He couldn't raise a couple of thousand dollars on short notice and not ninety thousand on any notice at all, and I'm sure that's not just hearsay."

"Why couldn't he? Maurice described him as a strange bird."

"Well, he and I were members of the same men's club and the treasurer of the club told me, confidentially of course, that André had been dropped from the membership roles for nonpayment of dues."

"Maybe he got tired of looking at the same hands clutching the daily newspaper."

Fleming shook his head. "It's the money."

"What happened to his wife?"

"Died in childbirth."

"The only child?" He nodded, looking strangely preoccupied.

"Where's your son, Fleming?"

His head jerked up. "I thought we were trying to get to the bottom of this Garber business."

"We are."

"Well, I don't think a discussion of families is pertinent."

"Pertinence is relative," I said.

"Not my son, Rafferty. A discussion of my son is not pertinent."

"Since you hired me to do this job, why don't you let me decide what's pertinent?"

"Since I'm paying your fee," he shouted, fingering himself in the chest, "I'll decide what's pertinent."

"I didn't realize that your fee entitled you to play Watson to my Sherlock. I prefer to work alone. If I didn't I'd have joined up with Giarrusso's Security Service."

Fleming glared at me. "My son is living in New York now. He doesn't have anything to do with this and I want him left out of it. Do you understand?" He said it quietly, menacingly.

I got up. "I can find my way out."

I went through the foyer to the door. He started up the circular stairway. I was halfway out when he called to me from the top of the stairs, "And, Rafferty, you keep in better touch. I like to know what's going on blow by blow and that ain't playing Watson."

He disappeared. I stepped out but didn't pull the door to. Instead, I went back in and slammed the door from there and made a quick trip across the foyer and out of view from the stairway. I walked to the back in hopes of running into Mrs. Fleming. I pushed the swinging door to the kitchen. There she was, just sitting at the kitchen table.

"Mrs. Fleming, I'll be off now. Mr. Fleming has gone upstairs."

She gave me a big smile. "Well, I hope you two have gotten your differences straightened out."

"Oh, yes, indeed we have." I smiled back.

"Oh, good. Such a terrible thing about Stanley. I told Carter that I just couldn't imagine Stanley being dishonest, you know, about the books, that he must be in some trouble, but I never thought when I said that . . ."

"Well, you were certainly right. He was in the worst kind of trouble." There was an uncomfortable silence. She got up. "Don't bother to show me out. I just wanted to let you know that everything is okay. Look, I'll just go out this way." I moved quickly to the back door.

"Oh, no, Mr. Rafferty . . ."

"No, really, Mrs. Fleming, I insist. I wouldn't want to disturb Mr. Fleming if he's gone to bed." We smiled some more at each other. "I understand your son is living in New York now," I said conversationally as I put my hand on the doorknob.

"Yes, he is," she said pleasantly, like she didn't mind, almost like it was rather exciting.

I shook my head. "That's a big tough town. Does he like it there?"

"He seems to. Very much."

"Well, he can have it, for me. Too far away. You must miss him."

"Oh, I do. I know he loves it up there and I know it's selfish of me, but I wish he would come back. I worry about him—he's very young, you know."

"He'll come back, don't you think?"

She looked troubled. "I don't know. I'm not sure."

"Well, I hope you had a nice visit with him last week." I edged it right on by her.

"Oh, we did. He was only here for three days and then he and Carter . . ." She bit her lip as if she'd gone too far. "I'd hoped he would stay for at least a week, but he had to get back."

I could tell she was embarrassed. "I've spent some time up there," I said. "Where does he live?"

"On Broome Street."

"SoHo?" I asked and she nodded. "Isn't that a coincidence. The son of some old friends of my family is living up there, too, right there in SoHo. He's an artist."

She brightened up. "Really? That's what Carter's doing, too. I wonder if they know each other."

"I don't know. Why don't we put them in touch? Maybe they'll talk each other into coming home. I'll tell Jim to call him." Jim is a middle-aged detective I know in the Bronx.

"Carter refuses to have a telephone. That's one reason why I worry. I can't just pick up the phone and make sure he's okay."

"Why don't you give me his address? They can't live that far from each other."

She looked dubious. "I don't know. Carter's very determined to be completely on his own. He might think we're trying to check up on him."

"Maybe you're right. He probably has his own friends there anyway." I opened the door.

She put her hand on my arm. "Wait, Mr. Rafferty. How old is Jim?"

"Twenty."

"Well, maybe it would be okay." She gave me the address on Broome Street. "Do you think you could find out from Jim—without being obvious—what kind of place Carter is living in?" She laughed nervously. "It would make me feel better. I don't know why."

I told her I thought I could manage that. "When did Carter leave?" I asked. It was a little too casual. She gave me a peculiar look. "You know, is he back in New York yet?"

"Oh, yes," she said. "He's been gone a week. He left last Monday."

The coincidences didn't like Carter Fleming III very much.

11

Old Friends Getting Together

MY PLAN WAS TO GO BACK to the Euclid to call for a reservation on the first plane to New York in the morning, then go over to Grady's and talk to Murphy about the Boy Scout. I got myself booked on a seven o'clock flight and lay back on the bed with my eyes closed. I was just beginning to relax when the knuckles started pounding on the door. When I opened it I got a perfectly framed picture of Uncle Roddy with his eyes at half mast. A younger, more brutal looking man was standing behind him chomping on a wad of chewing gum. It took me a minute to realize who he was. His name was Phil Fonte, and he was the younger brother of Raymond Fonte whom I enjoyed beating up several times while we were at Redemptorist together. Raymond and I had it in for each other for some unspecified reason. When feelings ran high we would meet after school, each with his group of supporters, being careful to move down the street a good distance so the nuns wouldn't catch us fighting. Little Phil, still at St. Alphonsus, cried one day when I punched his brother in the face and spilled a lot of his blood. He stood behind Rankin now sneering at me. This damn town is entirely too small.

"Well, well, Lieutenant, what a surprise," I said cheerfully. Uncle Roddy always liked me to address him formally in front of subordinates.

"Mind if we come in, Neal?"

"Not at all, Lieutenant. It's always a pleasure to welcome officers of the law to my humble house." I stood back and made a sweeping gesture of entrance.

"Hm," said Rankin.

We sat around the dining table. "Can I get you boys something to drink? Coffee? Or how about something a bit stronger—if you're going to be calling it quits for the night soon?" I have never seen Rankin turn down a drink.

"A Scotch and water for me," he said. Fonte nodded agreement. I went into the kitchen and fixed two drinks.

"This is Sergeant Fonte, Neal. He's going to be working this case with me."

The only acknowledgment I got from Fonte was when he popped his wad of gum at me.

"Sergeant," I said and handed him his drink.

Rankin smiled at me, a tired, almost affectionate smile.

"Well, Lieutenant, your disposition seems somewhat improved since we last met. I suppose Carter Fleming is responsible for that."

The smile vanished. "Don't get snide, Neal."

Fonte spoke. "Why don't we take this guy in, Lieutenant. I'm sure he'll be real cooperative down at headquarters." Rankin shot him a glance that clearly stated shut up.

"Look, Neal, let's level with each other. If we pool our information, we'll get Fleming out of the hot seat a lot faster."

"I didn't know that Fleming was in any hot seat. You must know more than I do already. All I know is what Fleming told me. What did he tell you?"

"He didn't have much to say to us."

I chuckled. "I told you Fleming wasn't going to like you charging in on him like that. He likes things his own way. "

Rankin did a short deep-breathing exercise. "Hell, Neal, I know Fleming's big stuff in this city and has a lot of connections, and that a little guy like me should tread lightly and all that crap, but he's in the hot seat as far as I'm concerned. Look at it my way—he hires a private dick because he has some gripe with Garber. Garber is found murdered and so far we don't know of anyone else with a gripe against him. I ain't sayin' we got anything on him. I just want to know why he hired you. You wanted to talk to him, he wanted to talk to you, the Garber women are in no condition to talk at all and I've got a job to do. Hell, if you don't tell, then he's gonna have to and he ain't gonna like that one bit and I'll be the one to catch it if we have to bring him in."

"That might be fun to see."

He brought the glass that was halfway to his mouth down heavily, sloshing Scotch all over the table. "You gonna tell me or not, Neal?"

"Sure, I'll tell you. I'm just getting back for that dig you made earlier. You know."

His eyes got that dopey look. "Yeah. About your license."

"No. It was the dig before that."

He gave no indication that he knew what I was talking about. And he knew well enough that I wasn't going to say anything about Myra in front of Fonte. So I told him about the Blake editions. I told him I had gone to Garber's house, that Catherine had told me Garber had been missing for a week, and that it was the wife who hadn't wanted to go to the police. I said that I had talked to Catherine long enough to convince her to give me the key to the store.

"You know what happened after that," I finished.

"Are the books in the store?" he asked.

"No, and I don't think they're at the house, but I could be wrong."

"Why do you think the old lady didn't call us?"

"I don't know. The daughter said she didn't know."

He looked like he thought someone ought to know. "How come you're so sure those books aren't at the house?"

"I'm not sure, but it doesn't make sense that they would

be. Fleming called over at the house several times. If the books had been there, why wouldn't they just give them to him?"

"Maybe Garber stole them."

"I don't like that either. Like I told Fleming, it would have been a stupid thing to do."

"Stupid enough to get Garber killed." It galled me. He could imply that Fleming would kill for his books, but he never would admit that Angelesi would kill to save his hide. To him Angelesi had always been just a regular guy. It was Fleming's enormous wealth that made him a suspect.

"Well, Lieutenant, these are all just speculations. Right? What we need are some facts. Like what was Garber shot with."

"A .22." He finished off his drink.

I pushed myself away from the table. "If it's alright with you, Lieutenant, I'm going to New York tomorrow. I was hired to find those books and it's possible they never left there."

Rankin seemed to like that idea. It got me out of the way for a while.

I saw the gentlemen out. Rankin went out into the hall first. As Fonte passed by me, I said softly, "Give my regards to Raymond." He gave me a look that wished me behind a double set of bars.

I never did make it out to see Murphy that night.

12

The Man with the Mallet

IT WAS LATE AT NIGHT and dark. I was in New York City but I didn't know where, not even what section I was in. I couldn't see any street signs. All around me were old crumbing warehouses. And everything was deathly quiet. I had just run a block and stopped, out of breath. I didn't even know why I was running. My head hurt. I felt the back of it. It was pulpy with dried blood and my tentative touch sent sharp pains down the network of nerves in my back and shoulders. I tried to remember how it had happened or how I had come to be where I was. My thinking was foggy and the concentration made my head ache more. Suddenly my thoughts were interrupted by an animal instinct that told me I was not alone, the same one that had told me to run. I moved down the street a few yards and stopped, my body tense, nausea grabbing at my stomach, my ears straining for the sound that had aroused the instinct but unable to hear for the rushing of my blood. I leaned against a low iron balustrade fronting a building, my head bent down to make the rushing stop. When I raised it up again I could see a street sign on the next corner, but when I tried to focus on the letters, my eyes went liquid.

The sound again. This time clear, unmistakable, feet moving in my direction and the sensation of more than one person trying to surround me. More sounds of movement, but everytime I peered in the direction of one, another would come from a different shadow. I started walking, quickening my pace to get to the street corner where there was more light. I centered myself between the four corners, in the middle of the street and turned to face the street I had just run through, naked without my gun. I waited for a move by my pursuers. There was nothing, nothing but the deathly silence.

I stood tense and still for a long time, still hearing nothing. I turned and continued down the same street, the muscles crawling in my back. As soon as I had cleared the intersection by several yards someone broke into a run behind me. I wheeled around and saw a big man with a heavy mallet in his hands. He was gaining fast. I sped toward the corner, aware that someone else had joined the chase. Each time my feet hit the ground an explosion went off in my head. I rounded the corner, adrenaline pushing me forward. Another man with a mallet came out of the shadow of a building in front of me. I stopped, looking for an escape route, my throat pounding. I saw an alley behind a stack of debris on the opposite side of the street. I ran to it, hoping it wasn't blind, and kicked aside a garbage can blocking the entrance. There was a clearing looming up at the end of the alley. I got a feeling of exaltation that died abruptly when I reached the clearing and saw that I was pinned into it by surrounding brick walls. But the wall opposite the alley was lower than the rest, so with a swift running start I scaled it, with remarkable agility considering the shape I was in. From the top I could see another alley across an identical clearing leading to the street. I jumped down, the pain from my head bombarding my entire body. But there wasn't a moment to lose. I picked myself up and stumbled to the alley's entrance half blinded by the pain from the jump. As I stepped between the buildings a hand reached out and grabbed me by the shoulder with such force that my arm went numb. A hideous grin on a face I recognized bore down on me. The man I'd left on the floor of Lucy McDermott's apartment lifted a sober and sinewy arm above my head. As the mallet came down, I heard a ship's horn blast in the distance.

And I woke up. In my thrashing around I had knocked the alarm clock to the floor but it was still obstinately blasting at me. I pushed back the bed covers and leaned over to shut off the alarm, the cool air in the apartment chilling my perspiring body.

"Hell of a way to wake a man up," I muttered at the clock as I put it back on the bedside table.

With an effort I got out of bed and took a hot shower to take the stiffness out of my back and shoulders. I came out with the appetite of an Oregon lumberman, which reminded me that I hadn't eaten since lunch the day before. After a huge breakfast of bacon and eggs I started feeling more like a human being.

I dressed in my best dark blue pinstriped suit with matching blue tie and white shirt with nonmatching gun and holster and felt worthy of Barrow's Auction Exchange.

I rode the elevator to the lobby. When the doors parted a stoop-shouldered woman with a mass of red curls, each balanced on the edge of the one below it like a giant red plant growing toward the sun, got in before I had a chance to get out. She had on a crumpled blue dress and black stockings. I wondered what my apartment building had come to, decided I couldn't afford to care, and went out the back door to the parking lot.

I got in the car and drove to the airport.

13

Gumshoeing

I ARRIVED AT LA GUARDIA at ten-thirty after a tedious flight. Flying is not one of my favorite activities, but I find it relaxing under certain conditions, those conditions including flying in a straight line, not sitting next to a cigar smoker, and not having my ear bent. The particular isolation of being encapsulated at thirty thousand or so feet influences my disposition so that social amenities become irritable as well as boring. As usual, I got a gabber in the next seat. Most of them withdraw if you don't grunt in the right places, but this one poured forth a steady stream of life history into my oblivious ear and grunted for me. She was enchanted to have made my acquaintance, she said as we disembarked. She would have been enchanted with the company of a chimpanzee.

As soon as I got in the terminal, I headed for the phone booths and got Barrow's address from the Manhattan directory. That done I went out to the procession of Scull's Angels and other assorted taxis, glad that I didn't have to face the baggage claim. I gave the driver the address on East 62nd. Forty minutes and two traffic jams later I got out at Barrow's.

It was hot and, remembering that most New York buildings are under-air conditioned, I was only hoping for a decrease in humidity inside Barrow's. I didn't get the blast of cold air like you get in New Orleans, but it was cool and comfortable and strictly first class. A small group of dark-suited men and sophisticated ladies smoking long cigarettes talked in hushed tones at one end of the lobby. Men in black suits were scattered at significant posts. I stood just inside the door looking for confirmation that I was at an auction exchange and not a mortuary.

One of the black suits came up to me. "Can I be of assistance, sir?" he asked the way a butler would if he caught a guest snooping around the parlor.

I gave him a card. "Who was in charge of the auction about two weeks ago when the William Blake books were sold?"

"One moment, sir." He disappeared behind a closed door carrying my card with two fingers on the edge like he was carrying a dirty postcard.

The group of bidders at the end of the lobby ignored several sand-filled ashtrays, stubbed their cigarettes out on the immaculate tessellated floor, and went through a heavy double door. My helper came back.

"This way, please, sir." He led me through the same door he had just so carefully closed behind him, past a secretary, into a large office. After announcing me to a wiry man sitting behind a desk, he discreetly left.

"How do you do, Mr. Rafferty. I'm Roland Engels. Please, sit down." His clasped fingers flew off the desk and breezed through the air, showing off diamonds. After he watched with concern as I sat down and was satisfied that I had made it okay, he asked, "Now, how can I help you?"

I told him I represented Carter Fleming and asked him who was in charge of the auction in question.

"Well, ultimately, of course, I am in charge of everything."

"Fine, then, Mr. Engels, you know of the auction I refer to?"

"But of course."

"And are you acquainted with Carter Fleming?"

"Certainly. We are always very pleased when Mr. Fleming visits us. We inform him by mailed notices of all important auctions. He is especially interested in paintings and rare books—a fact of which you are aware, I'm sure. Exquisite taste. And his lovely wife. She is very fond of antique furnishings. I believe, if I'm not mistaken, that the Victorian period is her favorite." My hips uncomfortably remembered the Victorian parlor. "But," he cleared his throat, choosing the right words, "is there—has there been any—problem?" His reserve was touching. "I mean, if you are here, there must be . . ."

"Relax, Mr. Engels. This is a routine inquiry." By his expression you'd have thought I'd hurt his feelings. "Just a few answers to a few questions should clarify everything. Did you send the set of books personally?"

"Not personally, but, of course, I supervise all operations." Such a bureaucratic-minded person should work for the government, I thought.

"Do you know for a positive fact that they were sent?"

"Yes, I do know for a positive fact that they were sent."

"How do you know?"

He sighed. "Mr. Rafferty," he said with infinite patience, "let me assure you that we are an entirely reputable business firm and an internationally known auction house. It has never before been necessary for anyone to make routine inquiries into our methods of procedure."

"Call it a nonroutine inquiry if you prefer. But let's cut the fancy talk, Engels. You've convinced me that you are in charge, and that this is a reputable, international auction house. What I want to know, specifically, is how you sent the Blake books to one Carter Fleming of New Orleans. And what proof you have that they were shipped. If that's classified as top secret under your methods of procedure, maybe I should go to the Pentagon for clearance."

I got a cold, nasty look. He pressed a button on an inter-com to his left and spoke into it without taking his eyes off me. "Karen, would you bring in all of the receipts for the books shipped to Mr. Carter Fleming in New Orleans. That would be about two weeks ago." We waited for Karen and the receipts in complete silence. He had nothing more to say to me, for the moment.

Karen whisked in playing Miss Efficiency of the Year, with her blue-gray hair flipped out on one side and tucked under on the other, her glasses suspended around her neck on a black cord.

"Here are the receipts, all of them, shipped August 15, the same day as the auction, Roland." Roland pointed the finger at me. She handed them over. "Is there a claim being made?" she asked me.

"No," I said. "This is a routine inquiry."

Roland's eyes closed in silent prayer. "That will be all, Ka-ren," he added to the amen.

I examined the evidence. All the receipts were there al-right. The books had been insured for five thousand dollars through UPS. Fleming also had them insured for appraised value on his own policy, according to the typed information he had given me.

Engel's hands slapped down on the desk. He pushed him-self out of the chair on them and leaned forward.

"If," he spat, "there is no claim being made, would you mind telling me what this is all about?"

I shook my head mournfully. "Gee, Engels, I'd like to, since you've been so cooperative and all, but discretion is of the utmost importance."

He looked at me in disbelief. "You mean you're not going to tell me?"

"I'd like to, really," I assured him, "but it wouldn't be—prudent." I got up and put the receipts on his desk.

His hanging mouth snapped shut. "Then, if that's all . . ."

"Not quite. Who was Fleming with at the auction?"

He didn't answer.

"Was he with his wife?"

Still no answer.

"Was he with his son?"

"Well, now, maybe I shouldn't tell you. It might not be discreet."

He started to straighten up smugly, but I grabbed one lapel. "One more time. Who was Fleming with?"

"His son," he sputtered. I hoped he wouldn't cry in front of me.

"That's very good, Engels. Thanks very much." I smoothed his coat. "You've certainly been most cooperative. I won't forget it." I left him shaking his shoulders and brushing off his lapel.

I stuck my head into the auction room before I left. The auctioneer asked quietly who would start the bidding for a crusty closed chest at an outrageously high figure. A hand raised, a head nodded, a folded magazine lifted thirty degrees by the side of an aisle chair. The low voice said the price had gone up three thousand dollars.

14

Chase Manhattan Jones

THE CABBY WHO PICKED ME UP outside Barrow's wound over to Seventh Avenue in silence. The drive was relatively uneventful, the qualification being lane changes only at the slimmest opportunity and slamming of brakes at red lights that had turned red a block away. I was on the verge of figuring that I would make it to Broome Street in one piece when the cab pulled up to a red light at 42nd Street. The driver must have seen something that riled him because he started expounding on life in the jungle and the unsavory types inhabiting what he considered to be his backyard. I wouldn't go as far as to say that what he was commenting on didn't have a certain glimmer of truth, it's just that I wasn't listening—I was too busy keeping myself upright on the seat. He was talking at me through the protective shield that, as one guy told me a few years back, keeps the passenger from robbing the driver and the driver from molesting the passenger, craning his neck around so that I could hear him through the hole on the side. He swerved to avoid an opening car door, barely missing the cab in the next lane. He slipped into a hole between two fenders, passed the car ahead of us, moved back into the same lane, and slammed on his brakes to keep from plowing into the back of a truck that had abruptly stopped in front of us. At that point he interrupted his monologue long enough to curse at the truck driver and change lanes again, missing a parked car by inches. So that I wouldn't dwell on the tenuousness of existence, I tried to calculate how many extra miles a day the twelve thousand cabs in the city add to their meters by constantly changing lanes.

We were passing through Greenwich Village, rapidly approaching SoHo where Carter Fleming's Broome Street address was located. The building facades had begun to change. We made a turn and there were rows of iron-fronted ex-warehouses that had either been fixed up into loft apartments or still looked uninhabited.

I got out of the cab and looked up at the building. It was one of the ones that seemed to have barely made it through the last war. The only signs of life were some stricken plant specimens peeking out from the third floor windows. I clacked up the iron steps to the door. There were no bells and only one locked mailbox with no name on it. I banged on the iron door knowing that I wouldn't get an answer and I didn't. I stepped back and cupped my hands around my mouth and yelled Fleming's name. That didn't get me anywhere either. I sat down on the platform to wait. I waited for about twenty minutes, periodically getting up to waste lung power on Fleming's name, and finally I heard the inside bolt sliding. A paint-spattered girl opened the door. I told her I was looking for Carter Fleming and asked her if she knew where he lived in the building. She told me he lived on the fourth floor. I thanked her and started to climb.

After a few deep breaths at the top I rapped on the rickety wooden door. From the other side I heard what sounded like somebody blustering around moving furniture. I had to knock again before I was heard above the racket. The door opened.

"I don't know you." The smell of beer and the voice came from behind a mass of dark hair that obscured what might have been an okay face if I could have seen it. He turned and pushed the door shut in one movement. I caught it but he didn't take notice of that. He kept going across the wide expanse of the loft to the refrigerator and took out another beer. I knew he didn't know me but I didn't know how he knew unless he was using a periscope.

I glanced around while he drained off half the beer. Wood debris and pieces of twisted metal were stacked in the back across from the kitchen area which consisted of the refrigerator, a stove, a sink and drainboard miraculously clinging to the wall, and a table with four chairs. The entire middle area of the loft was occupied by a mattress shoved up against the wall, with painted canvas hanging and leaning on the rest of the available space. While my apparently unwilling host stood in front of the opened refrigerator finishing his beer and opening yet another, I walked to the front where an easel was turned to the light trying to come in through the grimy windows. A small sofa and two chairs spilling their stuffing were arranged around a white plastic cube, creating a most unusual living area that Mrs. Fleming probably wouldn't want to know about. A ladder led up to a bed loft. A couple of bookcases crammed with books and papers stood around. A few lamps with hand painted shades completed the picture. I walked around the easel to view the canvas standing on it. Swirls of color were piled on into weird shapes with, I supposed, hidden meanings. I backed up to the window to see if I was missing something and was still trying to decide if it was very good or very bad when my host joined me. We appraised the canvas in silence for a few moments.

"Terrible, isn't it?" he asked more as a statement of fact. I shrugged and grunted noncommittally, my interest having been transferred to the tattoo, as amorphous as the painting, exposed by his shirt which was unbuttoned to the navel. "Well, go on," he growled, "say it's terrible if you think it is."

"Okay," I said, "it's terrible."

A laugh disturbed a few hairs. "Sold one almost just like it for a hundred bucks the other day. Wait a minute." He went through a door under the bed loft. I heard water running. When he came back his shirt was buttoned and his hair was wet and combed back. The face was okay, but if he was Carter Fleming III he must have aged almost ten years since he arrived in New York.

He looked me over with surprise. "I don't know you, do I?"

"I thought we'd gone through that. The name's Neal Rafferty. I'm looking for Carter Fleming."

"Friend of his?"

"By proxy."

"Hm. Sounds like his old man's snooping again. Look, maybe we'd better have a chat. Why don't you sit down?"

That sounded okay to me so I moved over to the chair with the least amount of inner springs showing. Like Engels, he watched with concern as I sat down. I was beginning to wonder if I had particularly catchy way of sitting down. Once I was in the cushion he smiled and gave a little snort of pleasure, like he'd really liked the way I'd done it.

"Shall I do it again?" I asked jumping up.

A few wrinkles of perplexity gathered on his forehead. "What?"

"Sit down." I flashed it up a bit this time by crossing my right leg over my left knee after descending. This was a mistake. I was so busy being cute that I temporarily forgot that a spring could be hidden by some of the escaping stuffing and, of course, thudded down right on top of one, painfully. Maybe his concern had been sincere after all. I managed to get through the ordeal with some dignity and once I was situated more comfortably I smiled up at him.

A half-laugh displaced the perplexity and he asked, "How about a beer?" I raised my hand to decline. He scowled.

"What's the matter, man, is it too early for you or do you need something more expensive?"

I got the drift. "A beer will be fine."

He made the trip down to the refrigerator and came back popping open the can. When he hit the sofa he groaned loudly and arranged himself more carefully.

After a long gulp he sat forward and began to speak earnestly. "I'll tell you, man, this is a hard life. Frankly, I'm overdue for a change. You see, I can't paint worth a damn so I have to work at keeping up the image, which I can tell you is harder than hacking with the paints." He shook his head and pointed with a finger. "This is not so for Carter and his girl. Because they're good. Real good. And they take it seriously which means it's a lot rougher for them. All I do is hack out a painting and take it up to Washington Square and play mad artist trying to make it to Tahiti or someplace. I put on a real show, swilling booze from a jug on the shoulder, getting drunk and proclaiming to the world that I'm too talented to cope with city life. The tourists eat it up and buy the junk. The locals know I'm full of shit but they bring their kids to watch. The kids think I'm better than a Punch and Judy show. People will believe anything you tell them if you're convincing enough. I try to impress that upon Carter and Lise but they're artists, not salesmen, and I guess the price they happen to be paying for the talent is poverty. It's okay, though. I manage to sell enough to keep us going. They'll make it if they stick with it 'cause they're that good. You tell his old man that and you tell him Chase Manhattan Jones said so. If that isn't good enough tell him to check my Dun and Bradstreet rating. It's still good—God knows how. Maybe that will impress him." He sat back looking depressed.

"You've got it wrong. Fleming didn't send me here to check up on his son. In fact, nobody sent me. I want to talk to Carter. Where is he?"

"No dice," he said. "Look, uh, what did you say your name was? Neal? Look, Neal, I like all the cards laid out. I'm not going to tell you where Carter is until you tell me who you are and why you're here. Give."

"I'm a private investigator from New Orleans. I want to talk to Carter before the police get interested in him. It might save him some trouble."

"Balls. It might get him some. Who sent you?"

"I just told you—nobody sent me."

"Balls again. Somebody sent you."

"Okay, okay. So United Artists sent me. They're interested in getting Carter to play a part in the new Paul Gauguin movie. Maybe you'd like the lead."

He laughed and rubbed his hands together. "Oh, this is choice. A private detective who cracks wise. You fit the bill alright. You're even good looking in a rakish sort of way. Choice, really choice." He stopped to do some more chortling. "Say, there, looks to me like you need some more hooch."

"Looks to me like you need it more than I do. It isn't necessary for my image," I said pointedly.

"No need to get hurt, now," he said as he shuffled back to the refrigerator.

"Did the old man hire you?" he asked handing me a beer.

"Yeah. But don't get the wrong impression. He thinks I'm in New Orleans. Is Carter with Lise André?"

"I need more before I start talking," he said sitting on the same spring. "Damn this life of poverty," he muttered. "Is the old man going to put the police on them?"

I shook my head. "He's mad as hell at the kid but I don't think he's that mad. And I take it Lise is here pretty much with Mr. André's blessing."

"Check. That's what you guys say, isn't it?"

I gestured impatiently. "You've got all the words down pat. Now all you need is a case."

"Looks like I got one—figuring you out. Let's start with why the old man hired you."

"What's with you, anyway? You in the protection racket or something?"

"Hey, this is my case. I ask the questions."

"Will an explanation get me the dope on where they are or will I just be shooting the breeze?"

"You get the dope if the explanation's good enough and if you mean what you say about saving them trouble."

I bolstered up with some beer. "Fleming hired me to find a missing set of books he bought at an auction. Somehow the kid figures into it. Maybe Lise, too. I won't know until I talk to them exactly how the whole thing stacks up. How I know all this I keep quiet, but if the police find out the same thing I did, they'll be after young Fleming pronto because a man has been murdered in New Orleans and the books being on the scene at the same time make the coincidence hard to swallow." I held up a hand to silence his protests. "None of this means Carter the Third or Lise had anything to do with the murder. If they didn't then chances are they won't even know it happened. But better me than the cops to find out first. That way maybe I can lend some protection, since Fleming is my client. Is that convincing enough?"

"Some stuff, alright." He stared at the floor for a minute then his head jerked up. "You better tell me how you know they're involved."

"Nope. That's not part of the deal."

"Then maybe I'd better talk to them first. Do you think Carter has the books?"

"Maybe you know the answer to that one and you aren't telling. What I think is writing in the sky. Are you going to tell me or not? . . ."

"No, man, you've got it all wrong. I don't know if he has those books."

"As I was saying before I got interrupted," I said, "are you going to tell me where Carter and Lise are?"

He sucked his lips in and shook his head. "I better talk to them first."

I stood up. "Sorry, Chase, but I don't like that idea. You see, I don't have a whole lot of time left and whether you believe me or not, I am interested in saving Fleming and his son some trouble. One way or another I'm going to talk to the kid today. And you're going to tell me where he is so I can."

He joined me in an upright position. "What if I won't tell you where he is?"

I took in some air. "There is an alternative to your not telling me, but if you're Carter and Lise's friend, you won't like it anymore than I do. The alternative is I call the police in. But I wasn't hired to turn my job over to them. That means you're going to tell me what I want to know. I don't mind getting nasty about it either."

He screwed his mouth into a sarcastic grin. "Does that mean you'd pull a gun on me?"

"There's that," I replied. "Now, let's have it. Where are they?"

"Hell, I don't know." He started pacing behind the sofa.

"I oughta punch you in the mouth," I said.

He slowed down and peered at me. "Look. How do I know if you're really a private detective?"

"Want to see my identification card?" I asked politely.

"Shoot, those things are easy to fake. How do I know if anything you've told me is true?"

"I guess you'll just have to take my word for it. I'm not fooling around any longer. Come on, you know where they are. Let's have it."

He put his palms up. "Really, I don't know."

I sighed. "That's a bad choice for a lot of people." I started reaching in the general direction of my gun. "Let's go."

He came around the sofa making conciliatory movements. "Cool it, man, just cool it. I *don't* know where they are, but I can find out. I know they're somewhere outside of New Haven. The deal was that when Carter came back from New Orleans he was jumpy as hell. I couldn't get it out of either one of them what the trouble was and I finally got sick of the little idiot pulling his nerves on me so I told him about a friend of mine who has a farmhouse up there and told him to go take a rest. He made the arrangements but the guy lives here in the city most of the time so I can find out exactly where it is. If you'll wait a minute, I'll go change my clothes and go with you. After all, I can't go around looking like a bum with a high-class detective like yourself."

I poked through the canvases while Chase scrambled around for what he called his business clothes. He went back through the door under the bed while I continued my survey. Lise André was very good and had a very distinctive style. Fleming's paintings were more abstract, a little like Chase's, but since I don't know much about it all I took Chase's word that he was pretty good, too.

I was finished looking but Chase still hadn't come out of the bathroom. I walked over in that direction. "Chase, let's move it. I'd like to be back in New Orleans tonight, not next week," I yelled through the shuttered door.

"Just a minute," he called over the running water.

I turned around to look the room over again. From what Chase had said, Fleming must periodically send someone around to check up on his son. It was no wonder that he didn't pass on the results of these findings to his wife. Her Victorian blood pressure probably couldn't take it. If any of Fleming's courtiers had stuck around long enough, Chase would have been glad to tell them it was a happy threesome; I wondered if Fleming knew about Lise and if it was the reason for his preoccupation the night before. Surely his thumb wasn't that interesting. It might have bothered me some more if I hadn't given up getting peeved over clients' lack of trust long ago.

I was still musing when something hard was shoved

against a vertabra in my lower back. My body stiffened. I started twisting my neck to get a view.

"Don't move." The command was enunciated very carefully. Water was still running in the bathroom. "Very slowly, and I mean *very* slowly, lift your arms away from your body."

I lifted them to flying position and a hand came around and relieved me of the weight of my gun. As soon as he had it he moved back.

"Now," he continued, "you may turn around, but move very slowly."

I turned. Chase stood there dressed every bit like a Chase Manhattan Jones should be dressed—in a dark suit, white shirt, and a conservatively striped tie. He pointed my gun at me.

"Shit. That was easy. Just used the old knuckle in the back routine and look what it got me." He jiggled the gun up and down. "You aren't so tough."

I didn't feel so tough. "Watch it. That gun's loaded."

He opened his eyes wide. "I should hope so." We stared at each other. "Now we play by my rules. I want to talk to Carter before you do."

I shrugged. "As you say, it's your game now. What's next? Are you going to tie me up?"

He nodded and smiled. "Good idea. Thanks." He stepped further away from me and sent quick glances around the room. "I don't think I have any rope. Got any ideas about what I can use?"

"Any nylon stockings around?"

He smiled some more. "My goodness, you're cooperative when you're looking down a gun barrel. That *is* a good idea." He opened the door to the bathroom very wide and backed through it. I was already standing opposite. He kept his eyes on me while he felt around and grabbed the knob on a small chest of drawers. He fumbled in the drawer and pulled out a wadded up pair of hose.

"I'm sorry to have to do this Neal," he apologized, coming out of the bathroom, "but I wouldn't be much of a friend if I let you at 'em without talking to them first."

"Think nothing of it. It's just the embarrassment that's hard to take."

He chuckled as he flipped the hose trying to get them to unroll. They wouldn't. His eyes flicked down to see what was holding them and stayed there just long enough. I grabbed his wrist and began to twist painfully. He made a few gurgling sounds and the gun fell to the floor. I let go and his other hand took the place of mine and felt for damage.

"Hey, goddamit," he yelled, "that's my painting hand."

I scooped the gun from the floor. "Well, it's *my* gun."

We stood there snarling and glaring at each other like a couple of kids vying for possession of a football. I couldn't stand it anymore. I started laughing and laughed like I was seeing W.C. Fields playing Ping-Pong for the first time. I collapsed on the sofa and naturally hit the same spring Chase had been having trouble with all morning. It hurt, but for some reason it struck me as hilarious and I started guffawing all over again.

Chase had fallen into the opposite chair in the same condition. He sobered up first and went off to the refrigerator for beer. He threw one to me and fell back into the chair. When I opened it, it sprayed all over my face. I looked up at him, beer running down to the front of my suit. He tried to swallow before he got helpless again, but he choked before it all got down and we both sat there with beer-soaked ties.

It took a while to establish control, mop up, and get back to the business at hand.

"Look, man, you gotta understand my position. I feel like I'm turning in a couple of kids, for Christ's sake!"

"But you're not," I insisted. "The old man is paying me. I'm on his side and his son's and his son's girlfriend's. Unless they've committed murder, I'll stay on their side. I don't know what else to tell you to convince you that I'm a good guy."

"Think of something."

"Nuts," I complained, "Okay, try this. Carter was spotted at the scene of the murder. That's what I know that the police don't know. If they find out, there's going to be cops swarming all over this place."

Chase stood up and flailed his arms around. "But how do I know you're not just telling me that?"

"How do you know I'm not the king of Siam? Think of it this way: Fleming's paying me to find his books and keep his name out of a murder case. But his books, his son, and the murder victim were all too close the day of the murder. He's mad at the kid, but he sure as hell doesn't think the kid's a murderer. He didn't want me to come here; he'd blow a fuse if he knew I had. What he and no one else seems to be thinking about are the consequences if I don't get to the kid first. You think about it."

Chase leaned his head on a closed fist and mulled it over. After a heavy-lidded meditation he said quietly, "Okay. I'm going to trust you." His voice got progressively louder. "But I'm going to trust you because every other person who's ever been around here for the old man has been a snooping social register snob who wouldn't have sat on that sofa and spoiled his St. Laurent suit for nothing." He wiped the slate clean.

I've been liked for some reasons and trusted for some of the same reasons and some different ones, but this was the only time I'd ever been trusted because I was willing to pin my tail on a sofa spring.

15

More About Fathers and Sons

CHASE STUCK TO HIS STORY about the farmhouse in Connecticut. He said he was going to have to look up his friend and get directions. We took a subway to midtown Manhattan. Somehow over the roar in the tunnel I was able to think clearly enough to start wondering again why a guy like Chase would take on two starving artists. I asked him how he came to be in the protection racket, what his interest in them was.

"When I met Lise and Carter," he told me, "they were really having a rough time. I had that big old loft so I moved them in. I guess I feel more protective toward Carter than I do Lise. She's pretty tough and she's a better artist than he is. He's having trouble coping with this way of life—it doesn't take you five minutes to figure out he's a spoiled rich kid—but I admire him for trying at all. You see, Lise doesn't need anybody's protection. She would have made it anyway. Carter won't, I don't think, not even with her. I think he'll end up going back home to daddy. Maybe I hope he will."

"So you put up with Carter because you like Lise."

"Yeah, I guess so. He can really be a little shit sometimes." He shrugged. "I suppose I'm just jealous of him, which is stupid. The girl is too young for me. Anyway, I've got to get out of this scene, but I won't quit for the same reasons Carter will. I like change and upheaval. And I know how to make money, too. It's just that all of it, the whole thing, is really beginning to get to me." His eyes shaded over with depression. Then he said in a low tone, threateningly, "You better mean what you say about saving them trouble."

"Watch it. You're being protective again and you're liking the girl too much. Why don't you find an older woman?"

"I need a lecture from a private snoop?" he queried.

"Sorry," I conceded.

It was well into the afternoon and I really didn't want this to be an extended stay. I told Chase to find his friend and get the directions while I went to the rent-a-car place and arranged for a car. I made the decision to let him go by himself on raw instinct which does go wrong sometimes. But this Jones character struck me as an impulsive type, impulsive enough to trust me for my apparently obscure sitting habits and equally impulsive enough to withdraw that trust if it wasn't returned. I watched him move down the street and wondered if I hadn't had better ideas.

I went into the rent-a-car place to make the arrangements and do some flirting with the girl behind the counter. After minor chitchat she told me there would be about a twenty-minute wait and I told her to send Mr. Jones over to the coffee shop next door when he came back.

I ordered coffee and sandwiches and tried to figure out what was going on between André and young Fleming. I couldn't quite see André using Fleming's son to steal the books, and, anyway, Garber must have let Carter walk out of his store with them. If, of course, the box the young man had been carrying contained the Blake books. And if the young man had been Carter Fleming III. That was the only way it made any sense. The problem was that I just didn't know enough, but I was laying money and my neck on the line betting that Carter the Third had some answers.

The sandwiches came and I finished mine, ordered more coffee and smoked several cigarettes. Chase still hadn't shown. But the instinct had been so strong. I realized that senility doesn't usually strike a person in his mid-thirties so it had to be that I was losing my touch. The consequences of such a thing happening were not pleasant to think about. I brushed it from my mind. After all, I hadn't been waiting that long. I tried to remember all the things I had heard about the virtue of patience but it probably wasn't a mere thirty seconds later that I began to get fidgety with the notion that a maniac with a tattoo was going to embarrass me for the second time in a day.

I lit what I had decided would be my final cigarette when he slipped into the booth opposite. He was sporting a new haircut.

"Time for a new life and a new image," he said.

"The little kids will be disappointed."

"There are other images for them. Hope I'm not holding up the works."

I told him to have a sandwich. "Did you find out where the house is?"

"It's all right here." He tapped his shirt pocket. "But it's a little bit farther than just outside New Haven. And my buddy says that he's not sure when they're due back. Hell, they could be on the way now." His tone was ambivalent.

"We go anyway," I said.

"I guess I can use some country air."

I paid the check and went to get the car. I asked for a Connecticut map despite Chase's insistence that he could get us there blindfolded.

"If you pass out," I told him, "I still want to get there." He called me a dirty copper for not having more faith.

Chase said he had two more stops to make, the liquor store and the deli. "We gotta get supplies, man. We can't go

way the hell to wherever it is we're going without supplies."
He came back with smokes, bourbon, and pastrami sandwiches.

"If these supplies are any indication," I complained, "a little farther outside New Haven means we'll be driving all
night."

"Just sit back and relax, Neal. I'll have us there in a couple
of hours flat." He lit a cigarette and we got on the road. I sat
back, but I didn't relax. I never do when I'm not driving.

"Chase Manhattan Jones," I mused. "How did you ever
manage to come up with a name like that?"

"I didn't, my parents did. They had a sense of humor."

"The name somehow doesn't go with the artist image."

"True. So I dropped the Manhattan from my signature
this year. But it was good last year when I played cards. Instant respect. My parents had the right idea; they wanted
me to start out on the right foot."

"Sounds optimistic, but is the foot on the right track? Artist this year, card player last year. What about the year before? Sailor of the high seas?"

He was puzzled for a second. "Oh, the tattoo. No, that's
part of this year's image. The wild hair, the booze, the tattoo. That's what I meant about keeping up the image being
a pain. Everytime I take a bath I have to put the damn thing
back on. It's a hassle, but the kids love it. Look, I'm getting
depressed." His shoulders fell and he looked straight ahead,
but the moment soon passed. "Maybe I'll become a private
dick in my next life," he said somewhat cheered. "This is
fun." I got passed a sly look. "Not bad the way I got your gun
away from you, either. With a little practice . . ."

"Yeah, but it might not always live up to your high sense
of adventure, like when you're sitting outside some fleabag
motel in the rain because a wife has gotten suspicious of her
husband. I don't understand why you don't stick with what
you're doing. You seem to be making out okay and maybe
you're not as bad an artist as you think you are."

"No can do. I always know when it's time to move on. I start getting depressed. Take this morning when I woke up. It was awful. When you came in I was on the verge of deciding I should be a businessman again."

He had an inner tension that always seemed to be coiled, ready to spring. And yet there was a certain composure even though he was in continuous movement. Maybe the movement kept the tension relaxed just enough, like vibrating a piano wire keeps it in tune. He was a person who would find adventure washing dishes in a hash house because he liked life and living; in other words, an eccentric.

"What kind of business?"

"It doesn't matter," he answered, playing with the knobs on the dashboard for no apparent reason. "I just look around and see an empty slot and move into it."

I would have tried his approach and picked a new life if I could have forgotten some of the details about the present one.

Two hours later, because of a hard rain, we had pulled over to the side of some rural road or other in Connecticut. We couldn't see where we were going which didn't matter too much because we didn't know where we were going—we were lost.

"I must have made a wrong turn somewhere," Chase said.

"Or two or three. Let me see the directions." Chase gave me a hastily drawn map that made about as much sense as my palm would make if I were trying to get to Moscow. I handed it back and pulled out the map I could read.

"If I just knew which road we're on now," he said, "I could figure out where I went wrong."

I had seen a hand-painted sign when we had made the last turn. "That's easy enough. We're on Manning's Road which must be a private road to some farm belonging to Manning."

I got an exaggerated look of admiration. "Gosh, Neal.

What astute powers of observation and deduction. I'll have to apprentice myself to you for a while before I strike out on my own."

"You'd have to pay me a lot," I said.

He pored over his map. "Simple error," he proclaimed. "I made a right when I should have made a left."

We waited for the rain to slow up, which it showed no sign of doing, ate sandwiches, put quite a dent in the bourbon, and talked. Nearly an hour later we found the farmhouse. We parked at the side and walked up on the open porch.

Chase rattled the door and called out, "Hey, Cart, open up. It's Chase. And friend," he muttered under his breath.

The door was opened by a girl whose beauty would rival Catherine Garber's when her face matured a bit more. Her chestnut hair fell to her waist and her large, dark brown eyes sparkled. She had on a smock. Several paint brushes showed in the long front pocket.

"Hi, Lise."

"Chase," she said with surprise, checking out his new attire. "What's up with you?"

"Lise, I want you to meet Neal Rafferty." She gave me her hand as Chase draped his arm across her shoulders. "Where's Carter?" he asked as we moved into a large, homey room with a low beamed ceiling.

Carter himself came out of a back room to answer the question. He wore faded blue jeans, sneakers, and had longish light brown hair. So far, so good.

"Right here, Chase. Who's the friend?" Suspicion clung to him like barnacles to the Lido Pier. Chase went through the intros again and Lise moved us over to some chairs and a couch and told us to sit down. When we were settled, she smiled at Chase and said, "Well, Chase, something's up to get you out of the city. I thought fresh air made you dizzy."

I took over. "Chase brought me here. I'm a private investigator from New Orleans." Before I could get out any further explanation, Carter's nerves snapped.

"You dirty son of a bitch," he shrieked at Chase. He jumped out of his chair with his fists clenched and his face contorted into a childish snarl. He crossed over to belt him, but Chase beat him to it and landed a blow on his jaw that knocked him down. I shouldn't have been, but I was amused.

Chase leaned over Carter and dragged him up by his shirt and threw him back in the chair. "Look, you insipid little bastard, you listen to what this guy's got to say before you go flying out of control again." He gave me a smile on his way back to his seat. Fleming rubbed on his jaw and Chase rubbed on his hand while Lise looked on horrified.

I tried again. "Carter, I was hired by your father, but not to find you. That's between you and him. He hired me to find his Blake books."

"So? So?" he yelled at me. "What are you doing here? I don't know anything about his stinking books."

"You know where they are because you have them."

He shut his eyes tight. "Get him out of here," he said threateningly to no one in particular.

"What you might not know," I went on, "is that Stanley Garber is dead. Murdered." His eyes popped open along with his mouth and he turned to stare at me. A muffled moan came from Lise's direction. If they were acting, it was a convincing act. "He was killed in his store the morning you were there."

"So?" His voice shook. "What are you trying to do, pin it on me? I don't know anything about it."

"Maybe not, but you were seen there and once the cops get that load, they'll be breathing down your neck every second of every day." I paused to let it sink in, but he stayed mum. I turned to look at Lise but she was staring at Carter. He wouldn't look at her.

She finally spoke. "Carter."

"Shut up, Lise." Her mouth clamped down and her eyes began to jerk around.

"Carter, I'd like to speak to you in the other room." She got up and walked out and after a moment's hesitation he followed.

There was some muffled conversation in a back room. I thought it sounded angry. It must have been. When they came back they were both wearing that clamped-mouth look.

"Lise," I said, "would you like to tell me about something?" She glanced in Carter's direction, got no response, vaguely shook her head, and stared at the floor. Carter braved a glance in her direction once she wasn't looking. Chase and I passed furtive glances. And so we all sat, everybody looking at everybody else. I began to get restless.

I stood up and took a deep breath. I was tired of giving out with the same old spiel so I thought I'd jazz this one up a bit. "Okay. Let's take it from the beginning. You, Carter, were seen at the shop the morning of the murder. In fact, you were so close on it that once the cops learn you were there, you will automatically be the number one suspect. Also, take into account the rather well-known story about your problems with your father and, hence, your money problems. Now, throw into that the fact that Robert André knows you have those books. And he'll tell all about it if he thinks it will save your skin from a murder rap. For some reason, he seems attached to you," I added. "Once he starts talking, he automatically gets himself in trouble for suppressing evidence. So does his daughter."

At the mention of André's name, Carter's head jerked toward Lise. She wasn't quite glaring at him, but her eyes had the intensity of Las Vegas lights in a nighttime sky.

"Seems to me," I went on, "that if you didn't have anything to do with Garber's murder, then neither did those

books. Once that's cleared up, you'll clear everyone connected with the books. I mention that in the event that you
don't care about your own involvement one way or another."

Lise's ferocious eye-hold on Fleming was slowly turning
into fear, but the kid still seemed unmoved.

I went further. "You know, Carter, you may not be overly
fond of your father right now, but he's the man paying me
and I sure would hate to have to turn what I know over to
the police. I would be throwing them my last lever of protection. I won't be any good to any of you after that. They're
convinced that those books are the motive in Stanley
Garber's murder and they're determined to pin it on someone. You're available and you're in possession of those
books. There's no way you'll be able to move them now." I
was getting a little far out on the proverbial limb, but I saw
Fleming's Adam's apple bobbing around in his throat. I
waited a decent length of time, but I got tired of eye lan-
guage. I went into my own act.

"Okay, Chase," I said, "let's go. There's nothing for me to
do but lay it on the cops." I started for the door. Chase
looked confused, but he played along and came with me.

"Wait." It was Lise. She hadn't moved, but she held out a
hand to stop us. "Wait." Her voice cracked and there were
tears on her long thick eyelashes. "Carter," she said anxious-
ly, "tell him. Please, tell him."

"God, Lise," he said giving her an imploring look.

"Then I will. I won't let them do anything to Robert." She
stopped, priming herself or waiting for Carter to do something, I wasn't sure which. She glanced back at me. "Sit
down, Mr. Rafferty. I'll tell you." Fleming put his head in his
hands. "Carter and his father don't get along well. Carter
wants to paint and his father wants him to go to school.
You're right, the main battle is over money. As long as Carter won't go to school, then his father won't give him any

money. Well, it is his money. Anyway, I think we can make it on our own." This last was said with a lot of pride, maybe too much, like she wasn't sure that they could.

"Don't go into all that, Lise," Carter interrupted.

Lise looked affronted for a moment, then resigned. "Carter took the books to sell them so he could get some money. But he didn't have anything to do with Stanley Garber's murder. You have to believe that. We didn't even know about it until you told us."

"How did you figure you could get away with it?" I asked Carter.

"I don't know. I really don't know." He was exasperated. Now that Lise had started the explanation, he couldn't resist a go at convincing himself and maybe me that foolish as it all was it had been necessary. He leaned in my direction. "Look, what Lise told you is true. I admit the whole thing was hare-brained, but my old man is being a real pig about everything. I was even sorry I ever told him where I was living. He sends men over to spy on me all the time and comes up here to bribe me into going back home with him. All I wanted was some time to get away from his dominance. He won't believe that I am a person with feelings and that I want to do something that isn't under his control. He has to control everything around him or he isn't happy. I guess I wanted to see him squirm for once and not be able to get something he had his mind set on, like the books. So I took them. Do you realize what a hypocrite he is? If I wasn't his son, he'd be buying my paintings, supporting me like he supports a bunch of no-talent idiots so he can see his name in the paper once a week. He can't stand to be out of the public eye any longer than that." He spoke with a bitterness that could only have been acquired over many years.

"I get the picture," I said. I got it all too well. Carter the Third and I had more in common than met the eye. The old man has his methods of control, too. It's just that he doesn't quiver quite like Fleming. "What did Robert André have to do with it?"

Lise opened her mouth to speak, but Carter wasn't to be stopped now. "Nothing. He had absolutely nothing at all to do with any of it except that I caused him a lot of pain by telling him what I'd done."

"Why did you give his name to Garber, then?"

"That was stupid. Complete stupidity. I called Garber to find out if the books had gotten to New Orleans. I told him that I was acting in behalf of someone who was interested in buying them. I was scared and nervous, so when he asked me who, instead of saying something intelligent, like my guy didn't want his name brought into it until he knew for sure that the books were for sale, I gave him the first name that popped into my head. Unfortunately, it was Robert's."

I bet he'd gone over that twenty times a day since he'd made the blunder.

"How did you know about that? Robert didn't tell you, did he?"

"Garber wrote André's name down before he died, probably while he was talking to you. Your name, too, only I thought at first it was your father the note referred to."

"Does my father know? God, what am I saying? Do the police know?" He looked frantic.

"No, not yet . . ."

Chase pointed at me. "You found the body and you took the note." He was gleeful.

I gave him a sly glance and he laughed. Carter attempted a smile which I supposed was relief.

"Then that means the police don't have to know about Carter at all, right?" Chase asked me.

"If, a chancy if and only if, I can find the murderer before they figure out it was Carter at the store. Those books arrived on the scene at the most inopportune time. So, Carter, let's have the rest of it. You left out a big chunk of explanation." He looked puzzled so I spelled it out. "Why would Garber let you walk out of his shop with those books?" Carter and Lise exchanged the furtive glances this time.

"That was between Garber and me," Carter said.

"And it will be between you and the police, and your father, if you don't give it to me straight." I disliked using scare tactics on him, but this kid was stubborn.

He stomped one foot on the floor and stood up. "No. That's it. That's all I'm saying. There's no reason for anyone to know anything more about it." He did a younger version of his father's angry quiver.

Lise smiled sadly at him. "I'll tell this part of it, Carter. If I'd never told you the story, all this wouldn't have happened." She looked back at me. "Stanley Garber is—was— my real father. I found out about a year or so ago, but I never let on to Robert. He may know it. I don't know, but I love him too much to hurt him by letting him know that I found out the truth. Carter is the only person I've ever told and he used it on Garber to let him have the books." She started to cry and Chase moved fast on the opportunity to comfort her.

Carter tried to look hurt but his anxiousness was too apparent. "It was a rotten thing to do," he acknowledged. "And it was stupid, too." He looked at Lise. Once he got a glance back, he continued. "I told Garber that I would tell all the wrong people if he didn't let me have the books. All he had to do was claim they had never reached him and my father would have picked up the insurance money. Then I could sell the books and everyone would be even except that my old man wouldn't have his books—" he really liked that part of it "—only once I got the books I got really scared because I didn't know what to do with them. How do you go about selling hot books?"

Chase started to say something but I shut him up with a sharp glance.

"Lise," I said, "tell me how you found out about Garber."

"I overheard it actually. Not too long before Lemmy left us I heard her telling her boyfriend about it. They were in the kitchen. I wasn't trying to eavesdrop; I just happened to be in the next room."

"What did she say?"

"She said I was Stanley Garber's daughter. She said that my mother had told her about it before I was born, that she had been having an affair with him. I don't know what was said after that. I got so upset that I left the house to think it over. I told Carter about it when he mentioned that the books were going to Stanley Garber's store. I didn't even know who Stanley Garber was. Carter didn't tell me he was going to do anything before he did it. I stayed here in the city with Chase while he was in New Orleans and he told me after he got back." She started to cry again.

"But I didn't tell Robert the deal with Garber, Lise. I swear," Carter said in a begging tone.

"Is that true, Chase, that she was with you?"

"The gospel," he said.

"Okay, Lise, take it easy. Who is Lemmy?"

"Oh Lemmy. That's what I had called her as a child because I couldn't pronounce her name, and I guess it just stuck. Her real name is Lucy McDermott. She stayed with us after my mother died to take care of me."

My head started to swim. So Miss McDermott's game was blackmail after all. "Why did she leave, Lise?"

"Robert couldn't afford to have anybody. We've been kind of broke."

"Have you heard from her since then?"

"Only once right after she left." She seemed hurt.

I established from Carter the exact time he had left Garber's store, him swearing every other sentence that he had left him alive. He said he had left the store by ten-thirty, probably a little before. He had the books with him at the farmhouse.

"Carter, I'm going to take the books back to New Orleans

and give them to your father. If you're lucky, the only trouble you'll get will be from him. The police won't want to believe that the books didn't have anything to do with Garber's murder. So just sit tight. If they show up to question you, tell them the truth."

"But," he protested, "that will make me a blackmailer."

"Better that than a murderer," I said.

"Can't they just hide out here until we hear from you that all's clear?" Chase's devious mind was taking over the protection racket once again.

"I don't know anything about it," I answered. We took the booty and left.

16

What Was Stanley Garber Thinking?

CHASE DIDN'T HAVE MUCH TO SAY until he did his navigation bit and made sure he'd got us heading in the right direction this time. I had insisted on driving. After the scene with the kid I needed something to hold on to, like the steering wheel.

But once we were off the gravel and back on asphalt, he started. "Okay, Neal, give. Who saw Carter at the store that morning?"

"Nobody really saw him, not to identify him, anyway. The woman next door said she'd seen a young man with long brown hair with Garber. Simple matter of putting two and two together after I heard the story about his problems over money with Fleming. Elementary, so to speak."

"You mean that what went on back there was a ruse? Nothing but a cheap trick?"

"The cheapest in the business and the most often used. You stick your neck out as far as it will go, camouflage it with a lot of gab, some tricks, scare tactics when necessary, and hope your hunch doesn't bite your head off."

"What would you have done if they had let you walk out?"

"Told you to faint when we got to the door."

"That would have been some show, old buddy," he chuckled. "Think Lise would have gone mad with concern? She is some knockout."

"It runs in the family. You ought to see her half sister." And, of course, that got me thinking about Catherine. I got her off my mind wondering why Garber would have let the kid walk out with those books. It would have been so easy to say that Fleming already knew they were there. Not only that, Garber would have had to sign for them when they arrived at the store. He must have known how easy they would be to trace. I didn't understand it. Unless he saw his chance to get even with Fleming for double-crossing him. And maybe he knew that the kid wouldn't know how to get rid of them and would eventually bring them back to save his skin with his old man. Either way, Fleming would worry over his deprivation, at least for a while. Only Fleming didn't know how lucky he'd been that the boy hadn't confided in Chase Manhattan Jones. I snickered out loud at the thought.

"You getting punchy thinking about the sister?" he asked.

"I could, but no, I'm thinking about what you'd have done if you'd known William Blake was sitting under your nose."

"Shoot, man, those books would be halfway to Turkey by now."

"Bull," I said laughing.

"Well, I would have thought about it. And I would have stormed around cooking up a dozen ways to unload them. But," he sighed, "in the end I would have told Carter to give them back. Hell, a man shouldn't have to pay for a sin twenty-one years old."

Chase sat back and opened the bottle of bourbon. "How about a little nip to oil the hinges, Neal? Get the load off your chest and let Chase Manhattan Jones, that well-known armchair detective, figure out who done it."

I accepted the bottle. "How could I earn my fee in good

conscience if I let you figure it all out for me? What do you think I am, a dishonest detective?"

"Yeah, I guess you wouldn't be holding out on the cops if you needed any help," he taunted and began to entertain me with the different ways he'd made his living in the past, digressing frequently on Lise André and wondering if there was a woman alive who could adjust to all of his lifestyles. He offered to bring the car to the rental agency so I dropped myself off at the airport. He told me he may have spotted his next slot and gave me a phone number where I could reach him or leave a message about the outcome of the case. I thanked him for the company, and he thanked me for the adventure and drove off to the next one, waving the empty bourbon bottle out of the window until I lost sight of him.

17

Still on My Case

IT WAS CLOSE TO 1:00 A.M. when I pulled into my space at the Euclid. I told myself that I was too tired to call Fleming, that it was too late. Of course it wasn't too late and Fleming would have been glad to get out of bed to be handed his books. The truth of the matter was that I didn't mind the thought of his having one more restless night. One Carter Fleming a day is enough.

Now that I was in the privacy of home, I wanted to take a good look at the reason Fleming was in a tizzy and at what I had been dashing around the country for. Not to mention what seemed to be a motive for murder. I opened the box and pulled out a volume containing *Songs of Innocence* and *Songs of Experience*. My hand glided over the satiny finish of the deep red calfskin cover. It was in good condition. I lifted the other six volumes which matched it in size and color. The bindings on a couple felt a little loose; one had a tear in the leather about an eighth of an inch long positioned so that it wouldn't show once the book was on the shelf. An outsized thinner book, *Illustrations on the Book of Job*, lay at the bottom of the box. I scanned the bumpy Moroccan finish and couldn't see anything wrong with it at all. I opened the book and began perusing the drawings. I was about halfway through when I was interrupted by a knock on the door.

I didn't have to be psychic to figure out who it was—the knuckles gave it away. I shoved the box of books under the bed and took my time getting to the front door.

"Good evening, Lieutenant," I said, counting on him not being asleep in a standing position. Fonte sneered at me over Rankin's left shoulder. "I hope this isn't your usual visiting hour, Lieutenant. I like to get some sleep every once in a while." I went on not inviting them in. They came in anyway and sat down.

"Sit down," I said to myself.

"You know, Neal," Rankin said, tipping his chair to a dangerously acute angle, "since you're John's son I really thought you were the different one in a breed of shysters pretending they're on the side of the law. I listened to your line about us leveling with each other—" that had been his line, not mine "—and I let myself believe that you were going to be the one in a million who would actually try to cooperate with the police. Instead, I find out that while you're handing me that line you're holding out on me. I find out that you're just like the rest of a bunch of no-good bums that call themselves private cops. To think I believed you might even try to make things a little easier, that at least you'd keep out of the way so I could do my job. No, instead you hold out on me while I got to tiptoe around so I don't make waves in the wrong direction. I got to play politics with the politicians, eat humble pie in front of the rich folks, watch out for the likes of you, and try to convince the taxpayer he's getting what he pays for. It's hard, Neal, it's hard and it's disappointing to have to face the fact that you are wrong in your judgment of a fellow human being."

"I guess it would be harder yet for you to believe that I don't know what you're talking about."

"I'll tell you what I'm talking about, Neal," he said, bringing his chair in for a landing and leaning across the table so he was in my face. "I'm talking about you not telling me about the McDermott woman. I'm talking about you going to her apartment knowing that I didn't have the information yet because I couldn't really talk to Garber's wife and daughter. And I'm also talking about how you broke into that apartment and knocked a man out to do it. That's what I'm talking about," he yelled at me.

"Do you mean to tell me, Lieutenant, that I should have been so presumptuous as to give you information that was sitting clear as day under your nose in Garber's ledger book? I guess I do owe you an apology," I conceded.

"I thought you didn't touch anything."

I didn't have an answer to that so I got up and put a bottle of whiskey and three glasses on the table.

"This isn't a social visit," he said. I started to remove the bottle, but he caught it in mid-air and poured himself a drink. Fonte the faithful follower followed suit.

He tapped his glass against his front teeth. "I'm going to let your illegal entry into that apartment and search of it go by this time, Neal."

"One second, Lieutenant. Since you don't mind my being presumptuous. Do you make it a habit to get your information from old busybodies who weren't even at the scene? She told me just like she told you that McDermott had left the day before Garber's murder. And that's where it ended. What she heard upstairs, heard, mind you, was Miss McDermott's drunk friend falling flat on his face with no help from me." I poured myself a drink and tried to look hurt.

He blew a lot of air at the ceiling. "Okay, Neal, we'll let bygones be bygones. I've got an APB out on her, but no dice so far. Also, there was a man with Garber that morning. You know anything about that?"

I shook my head. "Have you established a time of death?"

"The closest we can get is sometime around or before noon Monday. What went in New York?"

"We're minus a motive for murder. Fleming's son took the books."

"Jesus. What'd he go and do that for?"

"Near as I can tell, he intercepted them because he was mad at his old man. Rather childish, but that's what he did. I brought them back with me." I hoped he jumped to the wrong conclusion—that the books had been intercepted in New York.

He poured himself another drink and slugged it down in one movement. "I was counting on the broad killing Garber for the books. I guess that would have been too simple." He would think about where the books had been intercepted if the McDermott woman didn't surface soon.

"Maybe she killed him for another reason. But what do you make of her exit the day before?"

"Cover up. I think she wanted it to look like she was leaving. Then she stays overnight, kills Garber the next morning, and skips town then. Unless whoever it was in there with Garber that morning did it. But I've got my money on the broad. It all looks a little too convenient to me."

I nodded agreement. "Could be. Leads are getting slim, aren't they?"

"I guess your involvement in this case is over with, now that you've recovered the books."

"I've earned my fee, if that's what you mean. I'm still interested, though." I think I heard him groan. Poor Uncle Roddy.

18

Another Try with the Old Man

THE NEXT MORNING I decided to run over and see the old man before going downtown. I felt this urgent need that things improve between us. I'm sure it had to do with listening to Fleming's son the day before. I didn't like the idea that my relationship with my old man in any way resembled that situation. I had the Blake books with me. I thought he might like to hear about the case.

He was sitting at the kitchen table drinking a cup of coffee, and when he saw me at the back door he didn't spike the coffee or run off to the refrigerator for a beer. I thought that was a good sign. The house was quiet. The coffeepot was still on the stove warming in a pan of water. I got a cup and sat down with him.

"Where's Ma?" I asked.

He jerked his head toward next door. "She and Reenie and the kids went with Mrs. Tim to a wake. One of Mrs. Tim's friends. You know how they are, Neal. They're always up for a wake."

His mood was easy. Maybe what he needed was more time alone.

I pulled out the books and gave him some of the background on the case. I told him I'd had a hunch that had paid off in New York.

"Yeah. I talked to Rod'rick yesterday. He told me you went to New York."

I wondered what else Uncle Roddy had told him, but he wasn't saying anything so neither did I.

I told him about the trouble between Fleming and his son. It was a pointed conversation—I was interested to hear what he would say.

He shook his head. "What would he want to go all the way to New York for?"

I had just told him why the boy was in New York, but I couldn't expect miracles. I let it go on by. I told him that since I had found Garber's body while I was looking for the books, I was still interested in the case.

"Rod'rick told me you found Garber," he said.

"I'd like to find out where this Lucy McDermott woman is, talk to her."

"Rod'rick's got an APB out on her."

I wished Uncle Roddy would butt out.

"Yeah," I said, "I'm sure that'll turn her up before I could. It'd be a real coup, though, if I could do it first."

He agreed. I explained to him that at this point the best leads on McDermott were Catherine Garber and her mother, and that I was one up on Uncle Roddy because I had been able to talk to them before anyone knew Garber had been murdered. I told him that part of my interest in the case was my interest in Catherine Garber.

"She interested in you?"

I didn't know but I said she might be.

He nodded. "I'm sure she is, Neal. How could she not be? What surprises me is that you're interested in her."

I thought about that a moment. I really hadn't wanted to be with anyone since Myra, and I knew that he was making his general assumption that any woman would want me because I was a tough Irishman, but what I didn't know was why he was surprised that I was interested in Catherine. He might have meant that he was surprised that I was finally out to get any woman, or it might have been a slur. I knew the way he and Uncle Roddy talked. Uncle Roddy acted like the old man was still with the department. He gave him all the details of the "good" homicides. He had probably given the old man a pretty accurate description of both Garber women. And the old man might have been making a slur about me being interested in someone classy for a change. But things were going too well between us for me to jump to bad conclusions, and, anyway, I hoped he was right this time. I didn't care why she was interested in me, I just hoped she was.

We talked some more until I thought I'd better be getting the books over to Fleming's office.

"You still thinking about what I said the other day?" he demanded as I was leaving.

I nodded, just so I wouldn't ruin the morning. I would have considered things perfect if he just hadn't said that.

19

William Blake Finds a Good Home

I CALLED FLEMING'S HOUSE from the Channel, not expecting him to be there, but to make good my promise to Mrs. Fleming. She answered my call rather icily. I figured she had decided not to like me because she had told me too much but it could have been that she was one of those rare women who don't like to talk on the phone. I told her that her son wasn't exactly holed up in the Plaza Hotel, but that he wasn't in a tenement either, and that his roommate was a mature fellow who was going into business. I made Chase sound like a dedicated career type by insinuation, and I didn't mention that there was another roommate, female, nor that I had gathered the information myself. I did mention that the word was that her son was a rather decent artist. She didn't ask who I was quoting. In fact, she didn't say much at all except thank you and we rang off.

I parked my car in the garage of my office building and walked over to Fleming's office with the bundle. I entered a thickly carpeted reception room, decorated in muted greens accented with blue. A sweet brunette with curls falling softly around her rosy cheeks gave me the welcoming smile from behind her semicircular, completely cleared desk. I told her I wanted to see Fleming and she poked a fingertip that looked as if it had just been dipped in day-old blood at a button on the phone. In response, a striking woman of about thirty, wearing beautifully tailored clothes, emerged from an inner office. She introduced herself as Miss Taylor, Mr. Fleming's confidential secretary. Her makeup was perfect—so perfect that her face could have been cast in stone. Lack of facial expression intensified the image. Her amethyst eyes bit into my face.

"Mr. Fleming sees no one without an appointment," she said as if sneering at my colossal nerve.

I let my eyes travel at will over her handsomely cut suit. An angry flush strayed onto the cheekbones of her mask. I smiled. "He'll see me without one."

Air rushed through her nose. "I'll be glad to make an appointment for you, but the earliest possible time will be at the beginning of next week."

I shook my head emphatically. "You just tell him I'm here now."

"He's engaged on an important telephone call," she said. The air turned frostier.

"I'll wait," I said and slid the box off the brunette's desk and made for a low couch against the opposite wall. Miss Taylor waited until I turned back toward her so I could note the displeasure on her face before she went back inside. The receptionist and I did smiling exercises before she pulled out the paperback she had stashed under the desk.

And wait I did. The revenge of La Frigida. She finally appeared at the door and curtly told me that Mr. Fleming would see me now. I grinned as I slid past her. She flared her nostrils in response.

"Come on in, Rafferty," Fleming bellowed from the back of an office which would have dwarfed a party of twenty, "and shut the door behind you." I went to his desk, depositing the books on a corner of it. He was so busy writing something that he didn't notice that I hadn't come empty-handed. I tried to make myself comfortable in the depression of a modern white barrel.

He glanced across the paper-strewn desk at me. I'd been given friendlier looks before. "Go ahead with your report, Rafferty. I'll be finished here in a few minutes."

"Your books have been recovered." He slapped his pen down on the desk and showed me a lot of teeth. I gestured at the box.

"Goddamn good work," he shouted and came around the desk. He pounded me on the back and opened the box. He stroked the covers fondly. "Never thought I'd see these babies again. That was damn fast work, Rafferty. Damn," he reiterated ecstatically, caressing the *Illustrations* as if the book were a lover he hadn't seen in months. He stood so long with a lopsided smile of joy that I began to get embarrassed. He replaced the books in the box with a pat and faced me. "I want to hear all about it. Every detail. But first," he paused until he reached his chair and sat down, "there's the matter of your fee." He pulled out a check book and wrote ferociously, then with a pleased expression he handed me the check. It was for five thousand smackers.

"Thanks," I said.

"Well, I told you I would be generous if you found the books in a hurry. Less than forty-eight hours is fast by my standards, and I'm a man of my word, Rafferty. Now, tell me all. Who had them?"

He was going to hate it. "Your son."

He fell back in the chair as if a bullet had hit him and he was too stunned to feel the pain. The way his chest was depressed as he sat there made him look small and vulnerable. A flash of pity drifted across a few of my brain cells and found its way out again."

"My son?" It was a small voice, stricken with acute disbelief. He continued to stare at an invisible spot on the front

wall. When he finally remembered I was still there and I figured he'd had enough time for the news to sink in, I gave
him a rundown of the activities of the day before.

"Can he hate me that much? That he would blackmail a
man to strike out at me?" It was funny that from my objec-
tive rendering of the facts he possessed enough insight to realize that it wasn't purely a question of money.

"It was an act of desperation," I said for lack of anything
better to say.

"Yes, I can see that," he mused. "Rafferty," he said suddenly, "you don't think that—would he be desperate
enough? . . ." He trailed off, wiping beads of sweat from his
upper lip, his face drained white.

"No, I don't think he killed Garber." Unless he's a mighty
fine actor, I thought to myself, remembering that the time
of death Uncle Roddy quoted by no means cleared him.

"What should I do? Should I go get him?"

"Don't do anything. The police are busy with another
lead. Anyway, if they decided to look for him, it would take
them a few days to find him. They won't bother once the
murderer's been found."

Fleming, being a man of action, had to take some somehow. He made a speedy decision. "Rafferty, if you'll stay on
the case and find Garber's murderer, I'll double what I just
gave you over and above your fee and expenses." Now that
money was in the picture, he was his blustering self again.

"I was planning to stay on the case anyway, Fleming.
You've paid me quite well for what you hired me to do. Why
don't you buy one of your son's paintings instead? He wants
your approval more than he wants to hurt you."

I expected a tirade about minding my own business and I
wouldn't even have resented one. Instead I got a thoughtful
pair of eyes focused on me.

"Do you really think so? Maybe I'll do that." I stood up.
He came around the desk again and pumped my hand, patted his box, squeezed my shoulder, and gave me some other

signs of his approval. I didn't want to end up a mass of bruises so I extricated myself, closing the door behind me and arriving in Miss Taylor's office. She gave me a look that would have frozen the whiskey around a St. Bernard's neck.

"So long, icecap," I called to her, waving, and ducked out the door in case she decided to throw her office manual at me.

20

Somebody Don't Like Me

I WALKED BACK over to the office, stopping on the way for a cup of coffee and the *Picayune*. I was fumbling for my keys at the door when I saw the article. Curly's had burned down the night before. Details were scarce, but the possibility of arson was being investigated. I wondered where Murphy was today. Still reading, I scraped the Yale lock looking for the keyhole, found it, went to plunge the key into it and the whole lock fell on the floor. I dropped the newspaper and cursed my stupidity for having left my .32 at the apartment. Cautiously I opened the door, hoping that someone wasn't sitting behind my desk with my .38. No one was sitting behind the desk—it was turned over on its side. The waiting room was a shambles, chairs turned over, tables upside down, stuffing falling out of cushions. I picked up one of the tables to thrust with its legs in case the vandal was waiting on the other side of the wall in the inner office. He wasn't. He'd done his work and been long gone. The filing cabinets had all been knocked over and anything that was movable or breakable had been moved and smashed. Even my folding screen had been slashed. The smell of alcohol lingered in the air. Behind the turned-over desk was a broken bottle of Scotch. My merrymaker had apparently taken off with an unopened bottle of bourbon. It was the only thing that seemed to be missing. The metal cabinet housing my gun had been toppled but not unlocked. It looked like it had been beaten with a baseball bat. I summoned up my strength and put as much as I could back in order and called for the building maintenance man to replace the lock. Then I tried to get Catherine Garber on the phone, but no one was at home. I sat back and looked around the office; it didn't look so seedy anymore. Destroyed, but not seedy. I went through the mail and called the Garber house again, but still got no answer.

I waited around to try the number a couple more times, then I packed the .38 in its holster, taking no chances even on a seemingly innocuous piece of legwork. I went over to the post office in the area of Lucy McDermott's apartment. She hadn't left a change of address and I hadn't really expected the police to have overlooked the possibility. While I was in the neighborhood, I thought I'd go over by Mrs. Parry's and get the name of the landlord in case he had a previous address for Lucy.

I pressed the bell and waited for the answering buzz but didn't get one. A group of tourists on their way to the Café du Monde for morning coffee passed by, chattering about ironwork and cobblestones. In the midst of their clatter I thought I detected the flap-flap of Mrs. Parry's rubber sandals. I peered through the small iron grate in the door and saw her slowly making her way down the narrow entrance alley.

"So it's you, is it," she said as she stood on her toes to get a good look at me. "Did you bring any whiskey?"

"I promised, didn't I?" I held the Jim Beam up to the grating. The last couple of tourists straggled by as Mrs. Parry fumbled with the lock. Just as the door started swinging open, a gunshot exploded, wood splintering as the bullet embedded itself in the middle of the door above my head. I pushed the door open enough to slide through and shoved

Mrs. Parry out of the way. The women tourists were scream-
ing and scuttling down the street like a bunch of ferrets. I
drew my gun and took a tentative look through the grating.
Judging by the angle of the bullet, the shot must have come
from a second-story window or rooftop across the street, but
my vision was hampered by the design of the grate.

Mrs. Parry recovered herself from the bout of hacking
that had been brought on by the excitement. "Hey, what's
this?" she croaked. "Someone's shooting at you," she said as
if the first light of dawn had just seeped through.

"Sure looks that way," I agreed, craning my neck trying to
catch sight of my assailant.

"Haven't seen this much excitement since last night on
'The Rockford Files,'" she said coming up behind me.

"Look, Mrs. Parry, take the bottle and go upstairs and
calm your nerves," I suggested, even though she looked as
calm as a crocodile basking in the sun. "I'm going to open
the door a bit and see if I can spot anybody."

"And maybe miss something?" she demanded. "Not on
your life, Rafferty."

I started getting irritated. After all, I couldn't very well
try to draw the culprit out with her in the way. "Well, then,
move back there," I pointed toward the stairway. She drew
back not quite as far as I would have liked, but at least
leaned up against the wall.

I opened the door a fraction. Everything was deathly quiet. A few curtains flapped in open windows across the
street, but I couldn't see anyone in any of them. I opened
the door some more and started going out, gun first. A bullet whisked by my hand so close that I felt the heat from it.
There was nothing to do but retreat. I couldn't see well
enough to tell exactly what direction the shots were coming
from, but wherever it was, the person behind the gun had a
perfectly good view of me. I tried edging out again and
again a bullet smacked into the brick wall inches away from
my gun hand. I heard sirens in the distance and counted on

them drawing the attention of the assailant for a moment and dashed across the sidewalk, taking cover by a parked car. A bullet hit the concrete. I raised my head and peered diagonally to the right, which seemed to be the direction the bullets were coming from, judging by the angle of the last three. Another shot glanced off an iron pole supporting a narrow balcony. I ventured up to take a return shot and saw a movement on the roof to my right. Someone had quickly backed off. I stood up, aiming for the spot, but whoever it was had decided to leave, since the sirens were a bit too close for comfort and a getaway still had to be made. I tried to calculate where he would come down, but with the rooftops connected as they were, it could be on any of four different streets. I waited for the police, hoping they would be in time to surround the block and catch the would-be killer making his escape.

Police cars were suddenly swarming over the area. I walked down the street, still in the cover of the parked cars and with an eye on the roof. Several uniformed policemen jumped out of cars and took cover. I saw Rankin alight from an unmarked car on the corner. He saw me coming and waited, arms akimbo.

"Wherever there's trouble there's you, huh, Neal," he said as I walked up. Fonte, as usual, was leering at me from behind his shoulder, his mouth working hard on a piece of gum.

"I always like to be where the action is. But it's all over now. Whoever it was took his pot shots at me from up on that rooftop." I pointed. Rankin shouted instructions at the men to surround the area.

"Did you see him?" he asked.

"Nope. He managed to stay out of sight." He told Fonte to go down the street and ask the tourists if they had seen anyone.

"Any idea who it might be?"

"Who could possibly want to knock off a nice guy like myself?" I asked. He answered with a sardonic grunt and slung a thumb in his belt.

"Sure," he said, "some guy just sees your mug and decides he should take a few shots at you. Thinks maybe one might be lucky. Why? 'Cause he can't stand the sight of your face. Saw you from across a crowded cafeteria and just hated your guts."

"There are a lot of loonies running the streets, Uncle Roddy."

He stared at me through narrowed eyelids, made a few clucking sounds, and moved on down the street. I went back to where Mrs. Parry was incautiously standing in the open doorway.

"Did they get him?" she asked.

"Not yet."

"Somebody sure don't like you, Rafferty." She swallowed a small mouthful of bourbon and screwed the top back on quite carefully. I declined her offer to stand me a few during the afternoon movie and found out that she paid her rent to a realtor located on Royal Street. Before I could bid her a pleasant afternoon, she managed to cop the better part of a package of cigarettes from me. There just aren't many like her. She flapped back to her television set in the same red pedal pushers she'd had on two days before.

Fonte fell into stride with me as I walked back down to the corner.

"Did anybody see anything?" I asked to be conversational.

"Naw. Whadya expect?" He jeered at me and bit into his gum like it was the side of a pig. I'd liked to have shoved his head into some ironwork and watched him bray. "Don't you know by now that people don't never see anything? You must not be as smart as I thought, Rafferty." His lips smacked viciously.

"That's funny," I commented, "I wouldn't have picked you as the type that went in for mental exercise. I figured you substituted mouth moving for brain work."

He grabbed my arm in his less than viselike grip and stopped me. His shallow brown eyes glittered at me, betraying the kind of frustration that can be dangerous. "Play it safe, Rafferty, and button your mouth." His upper lip raised into a snarl so he could show me how tough he was. Somehow the tip of pink gum showing over the edges of his teeth spoiled the effect. I wanted to laugh but he's the kind who would plant something incriminating in your room. I started to move on. His grip tightened. "I mean it, Rafferty. Nothin' would give me more satisfaction than to see you buttoned for a long time."

"I believe you," I said.

We walked. Rankin came from around the corner.

"Anything?" he asked Fonte as we approached. He got a naw and a pop for an answer.

"Well, the boys aren't having any luck but they're still checking. Come clean, Neal. Why is someone showing you their fancy trigger work?" I could tell Uncle Roddy was worried about me, but was playing it tough in front of Fonte. I felt my attitude soften toward him and I wished I could come clean for him. I knew that telling him I didn't know was the same as telling him Mrs. Parry had a jealous boyfriend.

"Maybe I know something I don't know that I know," I said. His face was as blank as a cloudless sky. "What I mean is, maybe I know something that's important to someone else but I don't know yet that it's important."

"I got you the first time." He sighed. "It's your life, Neal. Seems to me you're not taking real good care of it."

"I appreciate your concern, Lieutenant, but I honestly can't figure the gunplay. Or why my office was vandalized yesterday."

He liked this new twist in the conversation. "Anything missing?"

"An unopened bottle of bourbon. It wasn't a search. A

locked cabinet wasn't even broken into, just turned over and beaten with a club." I didn't want him to get his hopes up.

"Seems that somebody don't like you."

"Yeah, that's what Mrs. Parry said, too."

"What are you doing in this neighborhood, anyway?" Fonte cut in.

"I dropped by to see Mrs. Parry," I said. "She's one in a million." Fonte gave one disdainful laugh and stabbed at the concrete with a foot the way a horse does.

"You know, Lieutenant," he said, "this guy's about as much on the level as the Rocky Mountains." He was sure being talkative today.

A police sergeant came up to tell Uncle Roddy that no trace of the gunman had been found. I told him I'd be checking with him and made my way over to Royal Street.

The secretary at the realtor's office wasn't too glad to see me. Her boss was out and it was absolutely out of the question that I look at the records. Didn't I know that was confidential information on the record sheets? I told her emphatically that I knew it was and eased a ten out of my wallet while claiming that I would never ask such a thing of her if it wasn't a life and death matter. She considered it as she moved the bill along the desk and slid it under the blotter. If it was really that important—I assured her it was—then she guessed it would be okay. She licked a finger and started flipping folders in a file cabinet. She extracted one and opened it up, licked her finger again and found the right piece of paper.

One glance told me that the information wasn't going to be worth ten bucks. There was her name, which I knew, the address of the apartment she wanted, which I knew, the previous address, André's, which I knew, and for references, André and Garber. There were a few other odds and ends like the fact that there was a shelf missing from the built-in bookcase and the toilet seat was falling off. Not exactly what I had hoped for, but it gave me an idea I hoped I could credit myself with having had in the back of my mind all along: Maybe André had an inkling of where Lucy McDermott was.

21

Lucy

ANDRÉ'S JUNGLE RETREAT was a bit more cheerful in the daylight. As I walked up the concrete path I half expected bright-colored tropical birds to flutter into the sky at the sound of my approach. The outside of the house was in worse shape than I had realized. Dark green paint that had been used as a trimmer was flaking off everything it had been painted on. Where white paint hadn't completely peeled off the body of the house, it had become a dirty gray. The shutters on the front windows were intact, but all along the sides they were either hanging by a few threads or had fallen or been taken down and leaned against the outside walls. Whatever money André had left had gone on the inside of the place. Or he was deliberately using the outside as a front, so to speak. I wondered if it really mattered.

I finished my inspection and pushed the bell. He came to the door wearing the same benign smile, only this time it was complemented by a textured shirt and ascot rather than the purple smoking jacket.

"My dear Mr. Rafferty," he nearly cooed at me, "how surprising that you should come back so soon after I practically had to toss you out for slighting my friend." He spoke with an inappropriate theatrical intonation, as if he had a tongue in each cheek. His eyes twinkled merrily and his smile had fractionally broadened.

"You can cut it, André," I said, trying to be tough but without being able to keep a touch of laughter from rippling my voice. "I had a nice long talk with your friend yesterday. I had to go all the way to New York to do it but he rewarded my ambition by coming clean. He even trusted me to return the Blake books for him. Surely that must make me a good guy."

"Perhaps," he said as if he didn't think it was possible, "but are you aware that I have had a visit from the police?" He posed the question like he was accusing me of some dastardly deed.

"The police do not take me into their confidence. Nor do I take them into mine. Which is why they came to see you about Lucy McDermott, not about the books. Am I right?" I felt like I was trying to sell myself for slightly more than he thought I was worth.

"Quite," he said stiffly. "You know about Lucy McDermott?" he asked with genuine surprise.

"I've known about her from the beginning, but your daughter filled me in on her connection with you. The police visited you because they, like myself, are trying to find Lucy McDermott and she listed your address on a form she filled out with the realtor she rented her French Quarter apartment from. I'd like a rundown on her from you, since you knew her for twenty years."

"I see," he said from far away. "So you met my daughter."

"Of course I met her. Wherever she goes, Carter Fleming follows. Right? Only she has a lot more natural sense than he does. It was on her prompting that he decided to quit being a fool and give up the books. She is also quite talented, André, and very beautiful."

It obviously pleased him that I thought so. "Well, then, I suppose I should invite you in now, since you have convinced me that you are indeed one of the good guys. "But," he said with an enigmatic smile, "I caution you, Rafferty, do not tell me anything it is not necessary for me to know."

I got the message. Subtle it was, but it came in clear. He knew that Lise was not his daughter, but he was better off not being certain if she knew. She seemed to know it would hurt him if he was certain. It worked both ways: She didn't know if he knew she wasn't his daughter and she didn't want to know. It may sound like a word game but it was two people's understanding of their own and each other's capacities and limitations. It was silent knowledge that an unavoidable and perhaps irreconcilable breach would be caused if the territory were ever touched. To each other they would always be father and daughter. My respect for both of them went up several notches.

André led me through the house to the very back room, one that had originally been an open or perhaps screened porch and had been enclosed in glass. It was a pleasant room accented in yellow, with a full back view of the twisted, dense foliage André called his gardens. André had been fixing himself a late lunch and invited me to share it with him. I gladly accepted. We settled ourselves in wicker rocking chairs on either side of a round wicker table. I glanced over at a white desk with a typewriter and several stacks of paper on it.

"My memoirs," he explained, following my glance.

"Is Lucy McDermott a starring character in them?"

"Not quite. Though necessarily she does have a minor part. I'm afraid I never cared much for her. Consequently, anything I may have to say about her may be rather twisted. I suppose I always blamed her for my wife's not loving me." He shifted his gaze away from the yard to my face. "That's not fair really, you know, but it's always easier to put the blame on someone else."

"You sound well aware of your prejudices."

"Yes, I suppose I am." He turned back to the view. "She was to blame in a very real way. I made a mistake when I allowed the situation to get the best of me and failed to handle it appropriately. Instead, I allowed myself to sulk childishly and, of course, lost my young wife's respect. I was not seasoned; my marriage to Jeannette was my first although I was almost forty-five years old. She was a very young, immature twenty-five. A charming girl, intelligent, but highly emotional. And so glib. Quite a match for myself in that respect. She was a great beauty, Rafferty." He screwed up his eyes as if he were trying to bring a hovering vision of Jeannette in closer. "Vivid, sultry brunette, but with those deep, wistful, honest eyes like a child's that touched my soul so deeply it pained me at times."

He paused and then sighed as if he had lost her. "Perhaps she married me because I seemed so experienced, so worldly. She cared for me the way one is fond of a funny old uncle. I knew when we married that she did not love me, not the way I wanted her to love me, but I felt that in time she would grow to. I hoped that, no I expected that our congeniality and special regard for each other would turn her fondness into love. Yes, I expected that." His usual light cynicism had crept over the line into bitterness. I could see no trace of amusement in his profile. His eyes seemed set in a spell and looked far beyond the backyard wall into another time.

Suddenly the spell broke and he turned amused, twinkling eyes in my direction. "You must think me a foolish old man who would bare his soul so openly to you, a stranger, and forget why you are here. I am setting the stage for Lucy McDermott's entrance.

"You must remember that I was indeed expecting my marriage to live up to the fantasy I had built around it. Perhaps it would have." He shrugged. "But I was never to know, for during that first year a mutual friend introduced my wife to Lucy and they formed a friendship that was actually quite enviable. They were inseparable. And constantly up to some mischief or another. Like a couple of children.

The house was always full of laughter. This did not exclude me," he added parenthetically. "In those days I was given a part of the fun. And then, let me see—how did it happen? Ah, yes, Lucy was to be married to a boy who lived some distance away or was away for a long time—I can't remember the exact circumstance. A short period of time, perhaps two months, before the wedding, she was jilted. She received a letter stating that he had found another love, he was sorry, etc. You know the story. Within minutes Lucy was here, distraught. My God, the hysterics." He paused as if the mere thought had made him weary.

"Anyway," he went on, "I must admit that over the previous few months I had grown to like Lucy, although I must likewise admit that I was a trifle jealous of the time Jeannette spent with her. But I wasn't that jealous, so when Jeannette sprang the suggestion that Lucy move in with us, it was only with slight hesitation that I backed the invitation. Need I say that this was the turning point?

"Lucy was always a handsome woman, never a beauty like my Jeannette, but striking. There was something subtle about her attractiveness that at times gave the illusion that she was quite beautiful. I can't exactly describe the phenomenon, but it had to do with—I know this will sound ridiculous—it had to do with her loss of vitality. Usually she was an exuberant, energetic person. When that energy became drained, like when she was tired or melancholy, then she would be beautiful."

He made a gesture of impatience. "It does sound ridiculous and it doesn't really matter. What was important about Lucy was her extremely compelling personality, her ability to make anyone like her. She could draw you into her web of confidence. You were certain that you were the only one who knew her secrets, and such exciting secrets they were. That was another of her attributes; she was able to tell the most insignificant event and make it sound as if it had never happened in quite the same, bizarre way that it had happened to her. She could entertain for hours with such stories, always managing to slip in a reminder that these things happened to her because she was a very special kind of person."

André paused to smile a small, embarrassed smile. "I'm not above admitting that this could well have been where the rub was with Lucy and me. As you know, I like to talk, too. It's hard to put a finger on the whys and wherefores even in retrospect. But after Lucy was well established in the household, things began to change between me and Jeannette, and within Jeannette, Lucy, and myself separately. The only thing that remained intact and stronger than ever was the women's friendship. Jeannette and I became ill at ease with each other. We even had a few words on a couple of occasions, something that had never happened before. Jeannette became more emotional, at times sullen, withdrawn, but only with me, never with Lucy, for Lucy only became gayer. Once she got over her unrequited love, and she got over it rather faster than I expected, she developed quite a passion for life. Her energy was excessive. Her taste in clothes became less conservative. She began to wear tight, low-cut blacks or bright, loud colors. Her makeup was applied, more and more heavily until it got garish. I daresay her taste in people changed as well, but this I wouldn't know positively because I became consistently less welcome on any outings until I finally became the fifth wheel. I even began to feel like an outsider in my own house. Naturally, I was resentful of such a state of affairs, but I couldn't decide how to handle it, and so I sat on the sidelines and watched Lucy teach my wife how to be the chic sophisticate, how to live; in short, how to like her drinks, and other things as well, tall and strong.

"I soon became disgusted with myself for my lack of decision and action, and I was on the verge of doing something that I sensed was rash, although it isn't clear, if it ever was, exactly what that something was. But before I was able to take this course, Jeannette got pregnant. Her pregnancy was hard on her and she was forced to halt her activities after the fourth month. Lucy, of course, continued to 'party,' but this is not to say the friendship lessened any, only it gave Jeannette and me some time in which to repair our relationship. We were happier in those months than we had been for nearly a year before. Unfortunately, Jeannette's health worsened and she became more and more prone to deep depressions. She died giving me our daughter Lise."

André had sunk back in the chair and was rocking it slowly back and forth as if he were in a fitful nostalgia. I felt that any comment would be trespassing on his memories and I hoped that he would not come back and realize with a shock that I had been there. It occurred to me that I was trying to shrivel into my chair and not breathe in my effort not to distract him. Finally I cleared my throat to ask a question I was more than vaguely curious about.

"Why didn't you let Lucy go then?"

He answered so fast that I felt foolish at having been silent for so long. "There I was, a man only a couple years shy of fifty. I couldn't very well take care of an infant alone. Lucy had seemed as distraught as I over Jeannette's death, although I don't think she felt quite the same sense of loss. Anyway, I did need someone to take care of Lise and I didn't know anyone else. Lucy begged me for the charge. I asked myself if I could, in fairness, blame her for anything. After all, Jeannette had a mind of her own. And, too, wouldn't I only be admitting my childish jealousy over her friendship with Jeannette? I tossed it around for a while and in the end I decided to let her stay, provisionally, of course. It would have been petty to do otherwise. However, it turned out to be a good decision. She was very good with Lise. Lise seemed to love her, and Lucy stopped being such an obvious siren, although she was never short of boyfriends. But Miss McDermott was no fool." He laughed with genuine amusement. "She wanted no part of any housework. She wanted to be my daughter's ersatz mother; she wanted to manage," he slurred the words, "the household. Really," he leaned sideways toward me confidentially, "I think she wanted to be the mistress of the household. But after I made it quite clear there was to be only one love in my life, my daughter, we stayed off each other's prospective ground and managed to live quite happily. Is she your chief suspect, too, Rafferty?"

I shrugged and envisioned Lucy as a siren once again. "Well, we do seem to be running out of characters in this case, but, no, I won't single her out for anything until I talk to her." I asked him if he had any idea where Lucy would have gone or where she had come from.

"Lucy never, that I can remember, talked about her past," he said. He furrowed his brow in thought. "I don't even remember her ever talking about relatives, if she had any. She may have told Lise something." I almost stood up and kicked myself for not asking Lise about that. And, of course, now there was no way to contact her without a few days' wait. I silently called myself the appropriate names. "I don't know if this will help," André added, "but another one of her passions was for Florida. She continually made trips there during the twenty-odd years I knew her. She and my wife went together several times."

"Do you know where in Florida?" I asked hopefully.

He shook his head. "No, Lucy never said where, unless, of course, she told Lise, and she and my wife went there during the time that Jeannette and I were estranged. Looks as if it's time for you to do some detecting, Mr. Detective," he said playfully.

I couldn't have agreed more. "Do you know if Lucy owned a gun?" I asked, but in my heart I was back in Connecticut asking the same questions.

"That seems to be the question of the hour," André remarked. "Yes, she did. Three or four years ago she got a bug and started carrying on something awful about how a woman wasn't safe on the streets anymore, and she went out and bought a gun for protection. The police, by the way, have extracted this information already."

"I'm not competing with them. Do you know what caliber?" Once again I was hopeful.

"No, I never saw it, but she said before she bought it that she wanted a small one that wouldn't be heavy to carry around in her handbag." A .22 would meet those specifications. "I remember because she carried on about it for days. But that was Lucy, always terribly dramatic." He started on his cynical chuckle but I interrupted.

"And she didn't bother to show it to you after all the fuss?" He shook his head. That was rather puzzling. "How did she react when you dismissed her from her duties?" If I started talking like André I would sound pretentious, I thought.

"Oh, I'm afraid she was quite bitter. I believe she felt she was being thrown out of the only home she had ever known. I told her that I would be happy for her to stay, but that I simply couldn't afford to pay her anymore. I was able to give her a show of my appreciation, but it was rather small. She pulled her theatrics on me, crying about how she was too old to get a job, which was nonsense, and I told her so and told her to stay at least until she got settled into something. But Lise was talking about leaving even then, and I think the prospect of the two of us living here alone was as bleak to Miss McDermott as it was unsatisfactory to me, so she left." He was beginning to look tired from his journey to the past.

"Did she know Stanley Garber twenty years ago?" It was my final question, but it was one too many.

"That I can't tell you," André said with finality. I got up to leave having about as much feeling for myself as I'd have for a snake. I'd asked a question that had a No Trespassing on it since I had arrived, a question that I already knew the answer to. I thanked him, rather lamely I thought, for his time and the luncheon, but he assured me that he rather enjoyed our little chats, although he would prefer that I would come back when I had something more pleasant than murder on my mind.

I realized when I left why I had liked him even when he was giving me a hard time. He really was a fine old gent.

22

I Want to See Catherine

I DROVE straight to the Garber house. The notion that I was getting warm on Lucy McDermott's trail was pulling at the back of my brain. André's story had created a fairly substantial mental image of her for me which, because of Mrs. Parry's description and the long reddish hairs I'd found in the brush, was of the forty-five-year-old Lucy trying to revamp herself into the younger sophisticated Lucy, the Lucy who was Jeannette's friend. I realized that Mrs. Parry's tongue would be rough on anyone who didn't oil it with a little liquor. There was a missing link and I was counting on Catherine or Mrs. Garber holding it. All it would take would be a little coaxing, a tug on the memory string and I would be finding out for myself who Lucy McDermott was and what she'd been up to. The question was, would Mrs. Garber be up to even a gentle tug.

I scrambled from my car and bounded up the path, anxious to find my missing link, an extra pulse reminding me that I was even more anxious to see Catherine Garber.

The gloominess of the house shortened my stride. It seemed more closed off than before, like the window shades had been nailed down, not just pulled. I waited a long time for an answer before I went around to the back of the house and exercised my knuckles there. A bird fussed at me from the top of a tree in response.

A car came up the alley and pulled under the carport next door. As I turned, the lady at the wheel averted her eyes and got very busy unloading groceries. I stepped over but she pretended I wasn't there.

"Excuse me." Her eyes darted like the sun glinting on a mirror and she ducked back into the car for her last package. "Have you seen Mrs. Garber today?"

I got another fast glint as she hoisted the bag and started up the steps to the back door. "No," she said without turning around. She slammed the door shut with a foot. Apparently this wasn't one of those neighborly suburban areas you get the hype about in the Sunday paper real estate section. My feet were glued. I shoved my hands in my pockets for added balance. A few seconds later the door opened a crack, then a little wider, wide enough for a voice. "An ambulance came last night." The door shut without a sound.

I walked back to the car where the atmosphere as well as the temperature was several degrees warmer and drove to the office. As I pulled into the garage Gabe made a tired jump off the conveyor belt and soft-shoed over to the car with a smile that showed off every white tooth in his black face.

"Hey there, Mistah Rafferty. Heard you had some trouble up there in yo' office." He pulled a toothpick that had already been reduced to a splinter from his pocket and started working on its total disintegration.

"Have you heard anything new?" I asked in a hushed conspiratorial mumble.

The smile vanished and his mouth drooped open, the toothpick supported by his lower lip. "Nothin' new," he mumbled back, shaking his head, opening his eyes wide and rolling them around by keeping them still and moving the rest of his face.

I nodded sagely. "Well," I said, "keep one ear to the ground."

I took the express elevator to the ninth floor with my favorite elevator operator, the one with a smile like Howdy Doody's who does a one-armed Hawaiian dance as the door glides open and shut.

Back in the office, I looked through the yellow pages. There was a little more than a column of hospitals listed. I leaned back in my swiveling office chair and watched a moth do its dance around the light fixture in the ceiling. I moved the phone in closer. I was getting ready to dial the first number on the list when one name stood out like it was printed in eighteen-point type. It was the Lakeside Hospital for Women. I dialed the number and asked for Mrs. Stanley Garber's room. After a tense silence I was told that she was in the intensive care section where visiting hours were ten minutes every two hours, for the immediate family only.

23

We Have Dinner

IT WAS GETTING LATE, but the traffic to Metairie was still thick and sluggish as a fat caterpillar crawling its way west. I got impatient with it and exited from the expressway on Bonnabel to finish the drive on Veterans Highway. The going wasn't much better, but there's plenty to look at, though the view isn't particularly scenic unless you happen to like a lot of neon. The buildings go up faster than an old building downtown can be demolished because most of them are prefabricated rectangles with a plastic facade that arrived intact on the back of a truck. But the signs in front of them are another matter. Everybody tried to erect one that was fancier and bigger than his neighbor's, with the result that you can see any one of them about as easily as you could spot a ping pong ball in a snowbank. And everybody's got a gimmick. There's a shopping center that isn't just a shopping center—it's a replica of a western town. Someone else had a cute idea for their castlelike bar. You walk across a drawbridge over a moat to get to the front door. Only the moat is always dry and littered with crushed beer cans and wadded napkins with jokes about the boy's night out and the office sexetaries who are pictured with long, skinny legs ending in points. Everyone was so busy being cute that they forgot about trees and sidewalks.

A kindly white-haired lady at the hospital's information desk directed me to the waiting room outside intensive care. There was no one waiting. I moved aimlessly around the floor, figuring Catherine had gone to dinner, and happened to wander into a solarium on the other side of the building. She was sitting alone in a corner near a window, her chin cupped in one hand and a book opened in her lap. I stood for a few moments in the open doorway watching as the last sunlight played in her hair. I sat down beside her.

"Hello," I said softly. Weariness pulled at the corners of her eyes. "What's happened?"

"My mother had another attack." Something like panic surfaced for a moment and displaced the weariness. "Too much strain," she said huskily and looked down at her long fingers spread over the pages of the book. They closed it and folded over the edges of the binding, gripping hard so that the knuckles looked large and white.

"How bad is it?"

"It's the worst one yet. They're being so careful about what they say to me that I know they think she won't make it."

I'm sorry wasn't enough and I couldn't think of anything else to say.

"The other night—after you left—the doctor wouldn't let the police stay," she said. "But they came back yesterday. I think that's what did it. So many questions." She sounded as if she were trying to muster up some fight, but it only chopped up her sentences and made her sound tired.

"They wanted to be thorough so they wouldn't have to come back," I said lamely. "Were you here all night?" She nodded. I pulled out a cigarette and put it in my mouth and took it out again. "Let me take you to dinner," I said as positively as possible.

She stirred in the chair and leaned her head on a closed fist. "I'm not hungry," she stated flatly.

"Well, you have to eat anyway. Not only that, I can't hear you if you say no." I said it with finality and put the cigarette back in my mouth but didn't light it.

She turned a mocking smile on me. "That was very forceful." The old belligerence swarmed up and flushed her cheeks. "Alright. But don't get any ideas because of the other night."

I started to say something in further reference to our passionless kiss that night and was counting on the cigarette being stuck to my upper lip. It wasn't and fell into my lap. I grinned. "Look. A man in my business has got to have ideas."

"Have you always got an answer for everything?" She stood up putting one hand on her hip and looked down at me.

"I try, but sometimes a certain face will even take my breath away."

"Oh, God," she said and closed her eyes, shaking her head.

I took her to a candlelit Italian restaurant with soft music coming out of the ceiling. Her golden glow had returned as soon as we were out of the last pale hospital corridor. We settled ourselves at a table and I ordered drinks before dinner. We both seemed agreed about getting the first one down before we went into any serious conversation. As soon as we were set up with the second round I asked her if she always had to be pressed into spending an evening out.

I got a very level look. "There have been few men I preferred an evening with to a decent book. I wish you would stop prying and being tough."

I raised my drink to her. "You are pretty tough yourself, Catherine." I ran my thumb down the index finger she had stuck out of her fist while making her prior statement.

She put her hands in her lap. "Are you still working for Carter Fleming? I told the police you were working for him before the doctor made them go away," she stated vindictively.

"No, and stop giving me a hard time or I might kiss you again right here in the restaurant." It was a bad joke or bad timing or something. Her face froze with anger or tension, but she relaxed as I went on. "I found the books in New York yesterday. His son had them. So I'm not working for him anymore; I finished the job."

"Oh." I thought she would be glad, but she seemed distressed again.

"I still want to find your father's murderer, Catherine. I want to help you. And your mother. Finishing Fleming's job just means that I'm not necessarily connecting the books with the murder anymore."

"Not necessarily? But what else could there be?" She put her palms up on the table. "Why would anyone want to kill him? I've gone over it and over it. Why?" Anguish started settling on her features. I ordered more drinks.

"Don't you find it strange that Lucy McDermott just disappeared the way she did?"

"Yes, yes, of course it's strange."

"Don't you figure that there must be some connection there? It's a little hard to take as pure coincidence, isn't it?"

"I don't know," she cried. The drinks came. She raised hers to her mouth before the waiter had it firm on the table and gulped from it. When she spoke she was calmer. "We've gone over this before—I have a thousand times since. I can't believe Lucy would kill him. I just don't know anymore."

"Do you like Lucy?"

"I like her well enough." Her cool and composure were in full force now. She made a small, impatient gesture. "Whether I like her or not really has nothing to do with it, does it?"

I didn't answer. "Would you like dinner now?"

"Order, but I want another drink." I complied, feeling the first three buzzing around in my veins and wondering if she did.

We gazed at each other across the table. "You don't tell much about yourself, do you Catherine?"

"What do you want to know?" she asked indifferently.

"Probably more than you'd be willing to tell without accusing me of prying."

She smiled at me. It was the first genuine smile I'd seen on her face. I felt rather pleased. "Probably," she agreed.

We talked for a while about the bookstore. She had decided to run it alone and said she would open up again after her mother was out of the hospital. She told me she liked the place and felt her best there surrounded by the books. All through dinner her soft, just-throaty-enough voice purred at me on the subject of books. I liked the sound of it and wished the piped-in tangos the Muzak seemed to be stuck on would pipe down. Her knowledge was extensive; an entire young lifetime had been spent accumulating it. It was as if she had cloistered herself within the walls and pages of the volumes, and a sad voice in my own mind told me it was all she would talk freely about. Over coffee I got back to the subject I was going to be stuck on until I found her.

"Catherine, there must be something, some offhand remark Lucy made that would give you an idea of where she was from or where she used to live and where she might be now."

She shook her head emphatically. "No, it's no good. I've gone over every conversation I ever had with her, which wasn't too hard because I didn't have that many with her, and I simply can't think of a thing."

"Do you think your mother might have some idea?"

"No, I'm sure not. We went over the same thing with the police. She didn't know."

"Well, your father must have known something about

Lucy if he worked with her for a year. You don't think he would have said something to your mother?" I was getting the feeling that there had been no real communication among the three of them which, as it turned out, was a pretty good guess.

That tension that seemed to freeze Catherine's face settled on it again. "My mother and father have what you might call a strained relationship." Her voice seemed to come from way back in her throat. "They always have for as long as I can remember." Her use of the present tense and the strange faraway depth of her voice startled me slightly. Her eyes got shallow, then deep as they dilated. She was looking through my face. I wanted to stop her.

I touched her forearm. "Stay here with me, Catherine," I said very quietly.

Her eyes snapped back and she was looking at me instead of through me. "I am here with you, but you're beginning to pry."

"We won't talk about it anymore," I said.

We left the restaurant and got in the car. Before I could get the key in the ignition Catherine said, "Maybe you should be looking for someone else besides Lucy."

I changed my mind about starting the car and turned in the seat to face her. "Like who?" I asked.

"Well, something happened about four months before Lucy came to work at the store." She was speaking very slowly. "I found a letter my father had thrown away. It caught my eye because it was addressed just Stan Garber. Someone could have been blackmailing him."

"Did you keep it?" She nodded. "Why didn't you tell me about this before?"

"I—nothing ever happened. I mean, it wasn't necessarily a blackmail letter, only it wasn't signed. I forgot about it until he was killed because I never saw any more. I worked on the books, too, and I never saw any money missing. Would someone kill him after all that time?"

"What did it say?"

"I can't remember the exact words. Something like, remember what I said and the person needing money and depending on their friendship. Then it said, your two daughters don't have to know about each other. And the person would be in touch." She stated it very matter of factly.

"Did it bother you?" I asked.

Her shoulders lifted an inch. She held them there and shook her head. "No. I didn't believe it." And I didn't believe her. "But it doesn't sound like the first or the last one, does it?" Her brow furrowed.

I told her I wanted to see it. She said it was at the house. We had an argument about whether she should stay at the hospital all night again and she finally agreed that she shouldn't, but she wanted to see her mother one more time that night.

I drove back to the hospital. There was a slight chill in the air that almost convinced me fall was on its way. Catherine stopped as we walked through the parking lot, her hands clutching her bare upper arms.

"Neal," she whispered, "I'm frightened." She didn't resist my arm around her shoulders.

24

After Dinner

CATHERINE'S CAR was at the hospital so I followed her back to the house after her ten minutes with her mother. Mrs. Garber's condition was still the same and that wasn't saying a lot for it, but somehow she was managing to hold on.

The air in the house was stagnant and hot. Catherine moved around adjusting thermostats. I sat down on the living room sofa and lit a cigarette. She came in with a cut-glass decanter of brandy and two glasses perched on a silver tray. She set the tray on the coffee table in front of the sofa and remained standing opposite me. "It may take me a while to find the letter," she said. "It's probably buried at the bottom of my cedar chest."

"Why don't I keep you company while you look?" I suggested.

"If you'd like," she said and headed toward the hallway.

I picked up the tray and followed her slim form in its silky powder blue dress. Her hair was pulled back and wrapped into a design on the back of her head. I studied it and her bare, not quite boney shoulders as she led me through the house. She turned into a doorway, switched on a light and we entered a large, sparsely furnished bedroom. The draperies and bedspread were cream colored. The floor was completely covered by a thick Oriental rug with a red and green border and oval center on a cream background. There were several dark wooden statuettes of primitive men and cats sitting on the low bookcases around the room, and above them framed pictures with brown and beige tones. I put the tray on top of a bureau and poured the brandy. Catherine went through another door that opened into a small dressing area with a bathroom right off it. She crouched in front of a cedar chest. I crossed the solid oyster carpet of the dressing room and handed her a glass of brandy, then went back and sat on the foot of the bed where I could see her as she unloaded woolen sweaters, old papers and magazines from the chest. After a while she took off her shoes and transferred her weight to her knees. She moved with the grace of a practiced dancer. I glanced around at the extreme understated attractiveness of the room. Except for the books, and maybe the cats, it was devoid of anything personal. There was nothing to give away even a small characteristic of the occupant.

"There must have been more letters than just this one, don't you think?" Catherine called to me. "Though it is strange that I wouldn't have seen any of them arrive, not even this one. I always looked at the mail first."

"Maybe the other communications were by phone," I said finishing off the brandy. I got up and poured myself a tad more which I didn't need. The house had cooled down, but I felt hot around the collar. I went back to my post loosening my tie and unbuttoning the top button of my shirt.

Catherine leaned back against the chest, stretching out her legs and crossing them at the ankles. She was holding a polished cherry wood box. As she lifted off its top she looked up at me. "It's in here," she said. I went over and sat beside her on the floor. She handed me a folded envelope and turned to place the box back in the chest. I took out the letter and read its short message.

Stan—

Think about what I said. I need some money and depend on your friendship.

There is no reason for your two daughters to know about each other.

I will be in touch in a couple of weeks.

It was typed on dime-store variety typing paper and had been mailed in a cheap business envelope. It was addressed to Stan Garber at the bookstore and there was no return address, of course. I started examining the smudged postmark.

"Well, what do you think?" Catherine asked impatiently.

"It must be a clue of some kind," I answered. Her head was bent close to mine as she looked at the envelope. I touched my lips to her temple.

"Is that all?" She moved her head so that our eyes were level.

I stuffed the letter in the envelope, folded it, and put it in my shirt pocket. "For right now," I said, and let my lips wander over her eyebrows. Her lashes brushed my face and I kissed her closed lids. She started moving her right arm away from me, but I clasped it at the elbow, planting kisses everywhere on her face but her mouth. She broke my hold and moved her hand to the back of her head and released her hair, her eyes still closed. As her hair fell forward, it hit the side of my face. I began to stroke it, feeling her cheek with my cheek and reaching for her hand. She cautiously twined her fingers loosely around mine, making no other movement. I put my hand on the back of her neck under her hair and kissed her very gently. Her grasp tightened. I kissed her harder, then moved back slightly to watch her face. Her eyes opened and looked at me like great gray lanterns. They closed again. She let go of my hand and moved hers to my arm. I smoothed her hair and ran my hands down her neck to her shoulders. I pulled her to me. Her lips parted as they reached mine. As we kissed, her hand found its way inside my jacket where it wandered over my chest, rubbing, caressing until it ran into my gun and holster. She held the holster. I started to move away so I could discard it, but her other arm had come up around my neck and held me to keep our lips pressed tightly together. I let her hold me there, my tongue moving deeper inside her mouth. I felt her remove my gun, her arm brushing past my coat, holding the gun off to the side. I slid my hand down her arm to reach the gun, but as I got to her wrist, she tossed it and I heard it thud against the opposite wall. The intensity of our kiss had lessened during the movement. I tried to take her back in my arms, but she pushed away from me and lithely lifted herself from the floor. She turned off the light and walked into the bedroom, stopping in the middle of it, her back to me. I went up behind her and put one hand on her shoulder, but she moved forward again, to the door, and switched off the light. The room went pitch dark. I stood still, trying to see through the darkness. My heart was beating hard enough to shake the house. I waited and heard a zipper moving almost soundlessly and material swishing lightly. And then her full, firm body was in my arms, bare and warm. My fingertips slid down her back. I imagined the trails they softly etched in her silky bronze skin. They stopped when they reached the small depressions right above her buttocks. I hadn't touched anyone like this for a long time. It seemed like I had been waiting all my life for her, but now that I had her, something a lot like fear was tugging at the base of my spine. The feeling drifted away as her hands weightlessly caressed my neck and moved down my chest and around my waist. We kissed full, strong kisses, pressing our chests and hips close to each other, until she took my hand and guided me over to the bed. She stretched out in the center of it. I could vaguely see the pale outline of her body and her hair spilled over the white spread. I shed my coat and tie and started fumbling with buttons, but she reached up and pulled me down beside her. I held her to me and my hand went over the curve of her hip to her thigh. Her breasts felt hard against me, her heart was beating wildly. I liked how solid she felt. I put my hand between her thighs, moving it up to feel her coarse, curly hair, then back to the smooth, bare recesses of her thighs. Her body started trembling slightly and then shaking. I eased the pressure between us and stroked her hair and back, but the shaking got more intense. She suddenly twisted away from me and sat up on the other side of the bed. I went around and sat on my heels. Her face was in her hands and every muscle was shivering.

I put my hand on her neck as if to stop the shiver. "Catherine," I said softly.

"Leave." The command was low and hoarse.

I held my position stiffly. My muscles felt like rocks.

"Please get out," she whispered.

I dropped my hand and rose like an automaton, the nerve endings dancing in my face. I picked up my coat and tie and left the room, closing the door quietly behind me.

25

The Scam

STUNNED IS THE WORD. It was a while before I realized where I was or that I was driving. I didn't want to think about it. I never wanted to think about it. Someone's hand lifted off the steering wheel and drifted to my shirt pocket, feeling the letter there. It looked like mine. I tried to concentrate on the letter, but it was no good. I kept driving, wandering aimlessly through the park at maybe fifteen miles an hour.

About a quarter of an hour later I managed to shake off the tentacles that had been clutching at my chest. My thoughts slowly returned to the letter and the idea that I had earlier started forming again like it was new. The letter had been postmarked in Gulf Breeze, Florida. Now I was driving with a purpose.

I headed downtown to the district headquarters to pay Uncle Roddy a friendly return visit. A group of cops was congregated on the corner. The neon map of the Americas on the side of the building was still winking the Alabama–Florida line, but they'd given up replacing the rest of the tubes long ago.

Inside the building it smelled as sour as a lineup of beaten suspects. The muscles above my lips flexed involuntarily.

Sitting on a high stool, the cop behind the small counter raised one eyebrow at me in question.

"Lieutenant Rankin in?" I asked.

"Second floor," he said, indicating the stairs with the side of his mouth, and went back to studying the scarred countertop.

Behind the swinging fire door at the top of the stairs was a small bustle of activity. Unnoticed, I went to Uncle Roddy's closed office door, knocked once, and stepped in.

Uncle Roddy had the phone to his ear, his huge bulk perched on a tilted chair behind a metal desk. "Call ya back later," he said into the mouthpiece, smartly righting the chair. "Well, well, Neal," he said heaving air through his nostrils. "What's new on the street?"

"Not much action to live up to this morning's," I commented. "Any word on the McDermott woman?" I sat across from him in a wooden chair.

"Naw. That broad's working a real neat undercover operation." He gave me the foxy eye. "What've you got?"

"Maybe something, maybe nothing," I said. "Have you got an APB out in Florida?"

"Why?" He put a slim cigar in his mouth, keeping his eyes on me.

"I hear she used to spend a lot of time there." He touched a match to the cigar's tip and the smoke drifted up into his right eye. In case I noticed things like that and thought it gave me an edge, he turned his left profile to me and fumbled with some papers in a drawer.

"Would it do any good to ask where you get your info?" He peered slyly over his shoulder at me.

"Same place you probably already got it," I said diplomatically. "Robert André."

The air whizzed through his nose. "You tailing me or something, Neal?" I laughed. The old fox, I thought.

We sat and smoked and gave each other amused expressions. I liked the way he wasn't going to tell me if he had the APB out or not.

I stubbed out my cigarette and slapped my knees. "Well, Uncle Roddy," I said rising, "it's been fun. I'll let you know if I hear anything else."

"You do that, Neal, you do that." He sat back with half-closed eyes and a smile like he was anticipating a geisha girl walking up and down his back.

I got to the door, put my hand on the knob and turned back like I'd had a brilliant second thought. "Say, Uncle Roddy, do you mind if I take a look at Lucy McDermott's things?"

"Come on, Neal," he kidded. "You trying to tell me you ain't never seen that stuff before?"

I smiled sheepishly. "Not close up, no."

"Well, then, sure, sure. Go the the basement and get Timmy to show you." I got the door open a few inches when he called, "And, Neal, if you find any clues, you'll let me know, won't you?"

"You got it, Uncle Roddy." I let myself out.

Timmy was an old friend from days long ago when I was on the force. His clipped white head was bent over a stack of green computer printouts.

I walked up to the desk. "Hi there, Timmy. It's been a long time."

He looked up uncertainly and then his face broke into a wide grin that was only partially filled with teeth. "You're right there, Neal." He stood up shakily and put a thin gray hand in mine. "What you been up to, Neal? How's the business?"

"Still making a living off everybody else's troubles," I said.

"And getting some for yourself, too, huh?" He wheezed out a laugh. Old Timmy had been in the basement since a bullet in the chest had taken him off the front line. He started reminiscing. "Yeah, Neal, you was some bullheaded young thing. How come you never laid off that Angelesi case when the Cap'n told you?"

"Like you say, Timmy, just bullheaded."

"You gotta lay off them politicos, Neal. They can put the pressure where it hurts. There ain't nobody big enough to play with them boys. You gotta learn that young."

"That's the problem, Timmy, everyone learns it so well that those boys can get away with murder."

"Yeah," he nodded knowingly. "Like Angelesi. The Cap'n, he sure was sorry to lose you. Said you was one of the best, but you didn't know how to keep your eyes closed."

It had taken the Crime Commission over two years to take Angelesi out of the big league. They had gotten him for taking payoffs, though, not for the murder of Myra. They were skeptical, too, and didn't even try to pin that one on him—it had been at least two steps away from him. But Myra had told me how Angelesi used to brag about his racketeering while they were in bed together. She had made the mistake of trying to squeeze a little more money out of him. She told me that, too. By telling me, Myra had her revenge. I raised enough of a stink—and there had been other accusations—that the investigation had been started, and Myra had made good her threat to ruin Angelesi after all. But that came much later. It had all started right before the elections and he had still managed to take the polls by storm. It was one of those things I never wanted to think about. The list was getting long.

"Timmy, give me a gander at Lucy McDermott's things. Rankin gave the okay."

"Sure thing, Neal." He looked through the green sheets, took out a ring of keys, and shuffled down the hall like he should have retired five years ago. "You take your time, Neal, and let me know when you go," he said as he opened the door. "The stuff is tagged on that right-hand shelf."

I pulled the door behind me. It was the typewriter I was interested in. I took a scrap of paper from my coat pocket,

wound it in the machine and typed some of the letters from
Garber's name and address on it. But not in order, in case
Uncle Roddy decided to check up on what I'd been doing. It
didn't take a magnifying glass or an expert to see that the
letter Catherine had given me had been typed on the same
Underwood. The serifs were all the same, the top of the *d*
was lighter than the rest of the letter, and the hump on the
n was broken.

Timmy asked about the old man and then we farewelled
each other for a while before I went over to Garber's store.
Lucy McDermott's two-bit blackmail scheme had me more
than curious. I wanted to see if she had fleeced Garber of
any more money than her three-hundred-dollar-a-week salary. If a job with a good salary was all she wanted, where
was her motive for murder? Unless she had wanted more
and on Garber's promises had waited around for it for a
year, realized he wasn't going to or couldn't cough up, got
demented over the fact, and killed him in a moment of fury.
I didn't much like the theory, but there didn't seem to be
any place to go for another one, and Uncle Roddy was sitting back waiting for her a little too calmly. No telling what
that old fox had up his sleeve, though.

Kids on dates and a few fancy ladies and gents moved
slowly up and down Royal Street looking in the windows.
Across the street from the store a wandering minstrel with
sunglasses on plucked at a banjo and sang like he was being
tortured. A sparse group of onlookers watched. I pulled out
the key Catherine had given me and slid stealthily into the
black, fetid shop. I didn't want to turn on any lights yet, so I
groped along the bookcases hunting for the hidden doorknob to the back room. I was ready to chuck the no lights
idea when my hand hit it. I swung the door back, went in,
closed it behind me, groped again for the string to the bare
bulb. Then I settled down with the ledger of monies paid
out. I started at the beginning. Lucy had been hired for two
twenty-five the previous August and three months later had

been raised to three hundred. The sum stayed stationary until the Saturday before she had left. I guessed Garber had paid her on Saturdays so that he could get some of his money's worth by at least having her show up for the larger clientele the weekend would bring.

There was certainly nothing outrageous here. I closed the book and put it back on the shelf and ran my eye over the rest of the ledgers. He seemed to have one for everything, money received, money paid, even a separate one labeled money for supplies. Not exactly a proper bookkeeping system. I spotted a spiral binding among the other books and pulled it out. It was a checkbook with three checks to the page and stubs. I riffled through the stubs. Most of them were paid to different London publishers. Then, the same August as Lucy's juncture, five hundred dollars had been paid to L.M. On the memo line was scratched bonus. I kept going. Three months later, November, there was another five-hundred-dollar bonus. The same the next month, a Christmas bonus. The next April Lucy finally hit some pay dirt, a thousand-dollar bonus. But the best was yet to come. One year later, on August 19, Lucy got a ten-thousand-dollar bonus. Garber had been killed on August 19.

"That old fox," I said out loud. So this was where Rankin's theory that Lucy had indeed not left on Sunday afternoon came from. It made sense in view of the fact that Garber had written her a check for salary on Saturday. Why not write the bonus the same day? But this only confused matters. Why kill a man who had just written you a check for ten grand? That was killing the goose. The same set-up would yield some more gold in a few months. Or had Garber written the check and pulled the final curtain? The whole bit was screwy, but wait calmly for Lucy to turn up I would not. It was Gulf Breeze or bust. Tomorrow.

26

A Bourbon Drinker

A STREETCAR CAME FAST down St. Charles Avenue. The driver had a sneering grin on his face, the kind you see in a comic strip, and probably with the same lines of drool if I'd been close enough. His foot was planted on the bell and the dings were coming as fast as ants out of a squashed hill. A wisp of a gray-haired lady sat in the rear of the car, one hand clutching the sash of an open window, the other clutching the flowering pill-type hat on her head. Her face was clamped tight with terror, but she sat very straight, holding on to her dignity as hard as she was holding on to her hat. Coming up behind the streetcar in a close second was a dark sedan sprouting arms and heads from its open windows. There were enough kids in it to fill a phone booth for a prize and they were shouting something that sounded like "Go, Sally."

I pulled into the passenger zone in front of the Euclid and ran to the telephone in the lobby. I dialed the police hot number and reported a runaway streetcar heading for Lee Circle. If I'd called and reported a murder, rape, or robbery, the broad on the other end wouldn't have winced, but she stuttered over this one and made me repeat the message.

Back on the street traffic was just beginning to unfreeze as the tip of the express trolley moved out of viewing range.

I circled the corner and parked in the back lot and went up in the elevator muttering what next, bunch of crazy kids, and a few other inanities people mutter to themselves when there's no one around to share a bizarre situation with.

The hallway outside my door seemed abnormally quiet, but it was probably just me taking my own "what next" seriously. I unlocked the door and before I even stepped over the threshold into the small hall to the living room, I knew something was wrong. I stood just inside the door trying to ferret out the difference while the tip of a cold finger moved ever so lightly down my spine. The thought slid across my brain that maybe I was reaching the age at which the events of a day take a toll on the nerves, but it slid right on out again because I knew why the hair on the back of my head was lifting. It was too dark in the apartment. Even with the door slightly ajar I could barely make out the outlines of the furniture. The window shades I usually leave open were sealed shut. A faint odor lingering in the air found its way to my nostrils like maybe the air system was pumping it out, but it wasn't, because the smell was the smell of sweat and it wasn't mine. I pushed the door to and went for my gun. It wasn't there. It was in Catherine Garber's dressing room. I crouched low and inched along the wall to the light switch. I reached up to lift the switch when from above something sharp hit the back of my hand and a hulk of a body was on top of me. The something sharp was a knife that the hulk was trying to stick through my ribs. As we struggled I was vaguely aware of the smell of bourbon coming through the smell of sweat.

What happened next happened very fast and I'm still not sure why I'm not dead. I was trying to get the weight off me without getting stabbed and without getting my neck broken. Right then a dull thud on the crown of my head accompanied a streak of red light. As the floor came up and hit me in the face, a woman shouted, "Stop it right now or I'll shoot!" I lay on the floor, fighting the temptation to stay there and rest in oblivion by twisting enough to flip the weight off my back, but the weight was gone and all I got for my effort was a glancing blow on the shoulder from the opposite wall. The light from the hallway coming in through the wide open door was dazzling. I got myself halfway up, but the floor came with me. After a deep, nauseous breath I tried again. I stumbled out into the hall with no idea in which direction I should give chase. I went back inside the apartment, wincing as the door slammed, and turned on the lights. Catherine stood there pointing a gun at me. The only color in her face was the gray-blue of her eyes. When she realized it was me, the arm with the gun fell to her side. I looked at her a few moments and felt the spot on my head with the springs underneath it. Then I took a long fall into the sofa cushions. I sat and stared at the blood oozing out of a cut on the back of my hand onto my trouser leg.

Catherine's breath caught sharply. "You've been hurt." She put the gun on the cocktail table.

"It's nothing," I said, getting up and going past her into the bathroom. I wrapped a hand towel around the wound.

"Don't you have anything better for it than that?" she asked close behind me.

"I suppose so," I said and wrenched off the towel. I reached for the iodine and bandages in the medicine cabinet. She took them away from me. Rather uncooperatively, I stood there glaring at her.

"Your hand," she demanded, her voice brittle. I held it out, childlike. As she fixed me up I looked past her into the bedroom, noticing for the first time that every drawer had been dumped.

"Friendly sort of guy," I said conversationally, in an attempt to relieve my own tension.

"Who was that man, Neal?"

"I don't know, but I wish he'd quit trying to terrorize me and stick around for a chat."

"Oh, is this a nightly occurrence?" She followed me into the kitchen where I dumped a short snort of Scotch down the hatch and poured two tall ones. The bottle of bourbon was gone. I wondered if that was what he had hit me with.

"I suppose the pattern could have been established if I'd shown up at my office while he was vandalizing it." I flopped on the sofa and put a drink in front of her. She left it untouched.

"How do you know it was the same person?"

"I'm counting on it. Otherwise there are two, maybe three people playing the same game."

"Three?"

"Assuming it wasn't an urban guerrilla sniping at me from a rooftop on Madison Street this morning."

"Have you ever considered a less hazardous form of employment?"

"No. What did he look like, Catherine?"

"I didn't see him."

"Boy, is he clever. Do you mind telling me how he managed that?" She stared at me with slitted eyes. "I'm sorry, Catherine. I'm being a jerk." I took two enormous swallows of liquor. "I didn't see him either. Look, thanks. I'm glad you were here. I mean, I don't know what he hit me with, but I think I would have been finished . . . Did he hurt you?"

"I thought you'd never ask," she said. "No, he didn't. He grabbed me from behind and walked me to your closet with a knife at my throat."

"How did you get in here?"

"The door was open. I heard someone moving around and called your name. I got a muffled 'Yeah' that I thought was you, but when I got inside the door, the lights went out and then he grabbed me."

"Did you think for even one tiny second that it was me?"

I asked her like I had only the most fractional hope that she could think I was so tough. The phone started ringing.

Her mouth curled up at the corners. "No, Neal, he was a lot bigger than you are."

I gave her a dour look as I crossed the room and picked up the receiver into which I growled a muffled "Yeah." Catherine shook her head and rolled her eyes upward.

"Rafferty? Robert André here. I've been trying to reach you all evening. I thought it might interest you to know of a few strange incidents that have occurred at my house since you left this afternoon."

"I'm all ears."

"Not more than half an hour after your departure I received a phone call that could only be classified as rude. A voice demanded, 'Put Lucy on.'" He imitated a gruff whisper. "Sounds like a cheap hoodlum, doesn't it? Nevertheless, I informed this person that Miss McDermott had not resided here for well over a year, upon which the telephone was slammed back on the hook. Perhaps an hour later the same voice called with the same request. I reminded him that I had already explained why Miss McDermott was unavailable, but that I would be glad to reiterate. This time he said, 'You'll pay for this,' before he slammed down the phone. Are you with me, Rafferty?"

"I'm right here, André."

"Just making sure. I do not like speaking over the telephone. I can never quite believe that the party I'm speaking to is really there. Anyway, I did not give much thought to these calls, as I imagine that you and the police are not the only ones hunting for Lucy. However, later in the evening I went out to dinner and returned to the most squalid mess imaginable."

"Is anything missing?"

"A bit of small change from the top of my dresser, but if anything else is gone, I haven't noticed so it must be trivial."

"Check your booze supply."

"How's that?"

"I believe that the same person left a calling card here not long ago in the form of a knot on my head. He's fond of bourbon."

"Terribly sorry to hear that, old top. Are you quite all right?"

"Quite. Interesting to know that Lucy has done such an ace job giving everyone the slip."

"So it is. Well, I'll be off now to check supplies. I grabbed for a bottle so fast when I saw the present state of affairs that I didn't notice if the stock was complete. I will resent it if this intruder imbibed my bourbon on such an unsociable call. So long, Rafferty."

"Give my regards to your frogs, André."

"But my dear fellow, I will, I will," he cried jubilantly and rang off.

I turned to Catherine. "Our friend has apparently been making social calls all evening."

"To someone you know who keeps frogs for pets?"

I attempted a laugh but it came out a snort. "Yeah. The man who employed Lucy McDermott for twenty years as a companion for his daughter—Robert André." I watched her face for reaction but there was none. She fidgeted for a moment with the strap on her handbag.

"Don't you want to know why I'm here?" she asked.

"I figured you would probably get around to telling me sooner or later."

"I brought back your gun," she said indicating the piece on the table.

"Lucky for me you did."

She flushed. "I came to apologize to you." She looked down quickly and started fooling with the strap again. What a woman. One moment so belligerent and outspoken, the next as shy as a budding flower. I didn't say anything. Her fingers stopped working on the strap and she raised her head. "Will you forgive me?"

"What's to forgive? I can understand that you might change your mind at the last minute about wanting to go to bed with me." It sounded cruel and I might have wanted it to sound cruel. I didn't know.

Her shoulders sagged. "I'm sorry. You must hate me," she said quietly. I thought she was going to start fooling with the damned strap again, but she didn't. She tried to blend in with the sofa cushions first, then she started fooling with it.

"Stop fiddling with your damn purse and come here." Her eyes opened very wide and her facial muscles petrified, but she managed to get up slowly, walk around the cocktail table, and stop about two feet away from me. "Catherine, I couldn't possibly hate you. What are you so afraid of?"

Her fright turned to misery as she stared at some spot on the wall behind my head. I stepped toward her. She couldn't retreat without falling over the table. "Why are you afraid? Are you—would it have been your first time?"

She shook her head sadly. "Don't think that," she said.

I wasn't sure what that meant, but I blundered on. "Are you afraid of me?" She didn't answer. "Are you afraid of all men?" She stared at something on the floor, like her feet. I lifted her head. "Did someone give you a rough time once?" She shut her eyes. "Catherine, I'm not going to pry, but if you had one bad experience it doesn't mean they're all going to be bad." I couldn't help myself. I held her and touched her hair, face, and neck. "You're a beautiful, intelligent woman," I said softly. "Men must want you all the time."

She smiled, but her body was stiff. "You're nice, Neal."

I shook my head. "I'm not any nicer than the next guy. Everyone gets carnal sometimes."

"No. You're nice. Really. You are."

I was exasperated. "For God's sake, Catherine, there's nothing wrong with being a little carnal sometimes. How do you know it isn't taking some serious willpower to keep from locking you in my bedroom overnight?"

"Is it?"

"Oh, for God's sake." I stumbled over to my drink and took a mighty slug.

"Well, is it?"

"Yes," I shouted. She started laughing. "What's so funny?"

"You are. And you really are very nice."

"Damn it. Come here." I didn't wait for her. I went to her and wrapped my arms around her and kissed her until the blood drained from my lips and we both needed air. "There," I said letting go of her. "That wasn't very nice and I enjoyed it."

I went into the kitchen and made another drink. I was getting drunk and I didn't care. She glared at me with clenched fists.

"Why do you always have to be so tough?" she said through her teeth.

I sighed. "I don't mean to. Really, I don't try to be." The old man loomed somewhere in my consciousness. I felt depressed. "Let's just admit it, Catherine. We just don't get along very well." I sat down wearily.

"No. No, that's not true." She looked upset.

"Well, come over here and have a drink with me."

"You're getting drunk."

"You see. Another reason why I'm not very nice."

She sat on the other side of the sofa resting her back against the arm. "Oh, Neal, why couldn't I have met you before?"

"Before what?"

"Oh, everything. It's me. I'm the problem. I give people a rough time, do terrible things to them, and then feel sorry for myself. I want things to be different with you." She stopped but her eyes went on, swelling with despair. Then they went blank before that strange and frightening depth took over. I let her go. She must have remained fixated like that for well over five minutes before her head dropped to the back of the couch. I didn't move. I watched her. I thought she had gone to sleep and bent over to take off my shoes. But when I sat up she was watching me. The despair was back as if she hadn't blanked out.

"What's wrong with a person who can't cry?" she asked.

I leaned over and took her hand. "Look, Catherine, you're probably very tired, and your emotions have taken such a battering over the past few days that they haven't left you anything to cry with. What you need is a good night's sleep. You take the bedroom. I'll sleep in here. And I'll fix breakfast for you in the morning."

She looked surprised. "Don't you want to come with me?"

"Sure I want to. But I won't. You've got enough to cope with right now without me. I'll be right here if you need me, but what you really need is to get some rest. No one needs to be crowded while their wounds heal. And after that, well, we'll have all the time in the world."

She stroked my hand for a few seconds. "I'd better go. I do need to sleep and I'll sleep better at home."

"I'll take you home," I said putting my shoes back on.

"No, don't, please. I think I need to be alone for a while."

I went downstairs with her and held her hand while we walked to her car. I opened the door, then took her in my arms and kissed her. She let her body fall against me. We held on to each other for a while, needing just to stand there together touching. She broke away abruptly and drove off waving. I think she was crying.

27

What Murphy Said

BACK UP IN THE APARTMENT, it occurred to me that I was more or less expecting the usual visit from Uncle Roddy and Fonte. As I sat there, I started feeling very destructive. I stood up with an urge to destroy the room and wished the bastard who had broken in earlier would come back so I could destroy him. I finally decided that a better idea than adding to the mess he'd made in the bedroom would be to go over to Grady's and hit some pool balls with Murphy.

Grady's was still crowded. All the pool tables were taken, but I didn't see Murphy at any of them. That was peculiar. I found him in the back, hunched over a beer at the bar.

"Hello, Neal," he said. He was listless, a little loaded maybe. His thin brown face, pointed and ratlike, was longer than usual.

"What's the matter, Murphy?"

He turned to me. "What's the matter? Haven't you heard, Neal? Curly's is gone."

I had never seen Murphy like this. I hadn't seen Murphy without a cue stick in his hands for probably fifteen years.

"I know, Murph. I read about it in the paper."

"Have you seen it? To the ground, Neal. I mean, Curly's is gone."

I told Grady to get me a beer.

"I don't know what to do with myself during the day," Murphy said.

"Why don't you just come here and play?"

"There's no one here, Neal," he said with disgust. "Grady can't hardly get his ass out of bed before two o'clock."

"Well, you can't sit around like this forever. You've got to find another place. What about that place over on Exchange Alley?"

"Bunch of screwballs and addicts over there."

"Speaking of screwballs, I need to talk to you about something, Murph. Remember the Boy Scout? That guy we played pool with over at Curly's the other day?"

"Yeah. The last day."

"Yeah. Well, I need to know everything you know about him, Murphy. It's important. I know his name is Louie. You got a last name for him?"

"Groz," he answered. He looked straight ahead. I knew there was something terribly wrong with Murphy when he didn't ask why I wanted to know.

"Where do you know him from?"

"Curly's."

"From how long ago?"

"I don't know. He's been coming in there off and on for the last several months. A nasty guy, but an easy five. He always cursed when he paid off."

"Right. I remember him doing that when he paid off the other day. What happened when he came back?"

"How'd you know about that?" Ah, a spark of life.

"I ran into him that night. He told me there'd been some trouble."

"I'll say. He came back in a coupla hours later and accused me of pickpocketing him. He said his wallet was missing after he left Curly's. Maybe so, but he sure had it while he was in there. He paid us off out of it. Right?"

"So what did you do?"

"I told him to eat it. He got so filthy-mouthed that Curly came over and tossed his ass out. Told him he'd call the cops if he bothered to come back." He shook his head. "Curly, Curly."

"Come on, Murphy. What else do you know about Groz? Do you know where he lives? Does he work? I need it all, Murph. It's important."

He talked into his beer. "I know all the four letter words he knows." He looked at me. "He's a drunk. He always came to Curly's in the morning and he was always drunk. He's lost all his coordination from drinking. He blows the easy shots. It's like he can't concentrate anymore. I tell you what, Neal, if that guy wasn't so crocked all the time, he'd be dangerous. You know what I mean?"

I thought I did. I asked him if Groz had ever brought a woman into Curly's or ever talked about Lucy. Murphy said the only woman he'd ever heard the Boy Scout talk about was some mother or another.

I stayed with Murphy for a while, drank several beers, and tried to snap him out of it. There seemed to be no way. He wouldn't even stand me for a fifty dollar game of pool. I finally figured he would just have to go through his time of grief.

I left Grady's more loaded than I needed to be, but I felt bold. And in no mood to go home.

28

Getting Warm

I WENT THROUGH THE SPARSE FOREST, the picture-book forest. Lamps glowed softly through the trees, but the houses and the spaces between them were dark. I got that feeling again that they were all unoccupied, unreal. I felt my attitude changing. It was never quiet like this in the Channel, but loud and crass and cramped. I knew my roots were still there, but I wondered if my heart was. I reflected on the effect of the booze in my system. It didn't seem like my heart should be thudding like it was.

Catherine came to the door with a robe wrapped loosely around her, her hair tossed from sleep, thick looking. She showed no surprise that I was there.

"Have you been alone long enough now?" I asked her.

"Yes."

I went in and kissed her like I was coming in from work. "I've had a lot to drink."

She looked at me without expression. "I'll make you some coffee," she said.

I sat in the kitchen and watched her pour water into a small drip pot. We didn't speak. Every now and then she would turn from the stove and look at me.

She sat across from me and watched while I sipped coffee. Under her watchful eyes, I felt compelled to say something.

"I didn't come here for coffee."

"I know." She put her hands together and rested her chin on her fingertips. Her body swayed back and forth slightly.

This time I led the way to the bedroom. We handled each other gently, a bit hesitantly, like neither of us had ever had anyone before. She didn't shudder or shake, but my quick first response left both of us trembling. We lay there kissing and stroking, first-time lovers still filled with desire, unable to rest. We lay there until I felt my blood soar again, and this time we got lost in it. There was no time, just the darkness, the dampness, and the way we moved. We fell away from each other, hardly able to keep our fingertips touching. I took her hand and put it over my heart and held it there.

We stayed like that until the cool air forced us to find the covers. She put her head on my shoulder and lay in the crook of my arm, getting warm. I didn't feel the least bit sleepy. I looked around the dark room, seeing the outlines of the bookcases. I thought I could see the pictures, the dark statuettes. I could feel the brown and beige atmosphere of the large room, so unfamiliar, so unlike any other room I'd ever been in. Territory that was not mine, the territory of the warm body next to me. I would enjoy the gradual feeling of becoming at ease in this alien atmosphere. I remembered when familiarity finally put me at ease in Myra's green and white bedroom. It had taken a long time because I couldn't get over knowing that I was not the only man who shared her most personal place with her. Things would be easier for Catherine and me. I had a place now, too. I thought about our time together there. I thought it might even be nice to move out of the Euclid, get a place where there were trees and a yard, more of a house. I thought about all the choices there could be. Catherine's breathing seemed deep and regular.

"Neal?" It surprised me when she spoke.

"Hm."

"It's nice like this, isn't it?"

"Yes."

"It's been a long time for me, Neal." The way she said it, I waited for her to go on, like she was going to make something clear to me. "What about you?" she asked.

"Yes. It's been a long time for me, too."

I waited again.

"Was it someone you were in love with?"

"Yes."

She didn't speak for a long time. I was starting to drift off.

"Why aren't you with her now? Why didn't you marry her?"

I thought about all the times I'd tried to make an honest woman out of Myra. "Honey, you're not rich enough," she told me. She had wanted me to buy her a house. So I lived at home, saving every penny. I was going to get her the biggest, finest house I could. "She's dead. She was murdered."

Catherine's body tensed. She didn't ask me any more about it. I turned to her and put my arms around her. We fell asleep that way.

29

The Milton McDermotts

WHEN I WOKE UP that morning Catherine was gone. She'd left me a note that she would be at the hospital and would see me later. I put my message under hers—I would be in Florida. I went back to the Euclid first to get my gun.

I decided to find out at the New Orleans post office what points a letter postmarked Gulf Breeze could have been mailed from instead of trusting my Chevy to get me to Florida before the post office there closed. I left with a list that included most of Santa Rosa County and parts of Escambia County and spent the better part of the next five hours on an irritably hot and uneventful drive east. Just mile after mile of uninteresting express highway that starts to roll a bit after you get out of the flat land New Orleans sits on. I bypassed Pensacola and the beach area by staying on the highway until I had to get off to get to Milton, the county seat of Santa Rosa.

It would have been easy if Lucy McDermott had been listed in the directory for either county or if she had a new listing, but those are the kinds of things a private detective does first that always add up to a big zero. There weren't enough McDermotts in either county to sneeze at, so I jotted all of

them down with their statistics. After all, Lucy's dead aunt
could be one of them just like she could be any other name
that was listed. After that I went over to the municipal
building where the records are kept and got a cooperative
guy there who liked that I was from the hot spot on the river and wanted to try to find me a clue. But first he wanted
to know the current status of Bourbon Street. And that only
after he had given me a rundown of the singularly swinging
time he'd had on the strip many years ago. He still had the
name of every joint he'd visited carefully filed away in a
prominent memory cell, along with the name of his favorite
stripper in each one. He chuckled, chortled, and snorted
over it all and finally got around to asking for the second
time what I needed. He went through some files and told
me that no Lucy McDermott had been born or married
there, nor had she died there, and that he sure would like to
do some more digging, but it was time to close and I should
come back tomorrow.

The first name on my Santa Rosa list of two was Avery
McDermott on Sycamore Street, Milton. I drove slowly
down the street past municipal row to a pleasant, tree-lined
avenue. There wasn't a gas station on every corner in Milton
and it took me a while to find one and get directions.

I passed through a section of Milton with old rambling
houses and cottages on spacious lawns. Then the houses got
smaller and closer together, and by the time I turned down
Sycamore Street, lawns were almost nonexistent and the
residences ramshackle. I found number 406 by a process of
elimination and went up the three steps where I noticed the
number, under several layers of paint, over the top step, underneath the screened door. A man in a white undershirt
and a fat cigar jutting angrily out of his mouth answered my
knock. He pushed the point of his belly up against the
screen, which put him about two feet away from me on the
other side of the door. He planted himself and grew out of
the flooring.

"I ain't answering no survey questions and I ain't buying nothin'," he said and bit his cigar.

"I'm not conducting a survey and I'm not selling anything," I answered. "I'm looking for Lucy McDermott."

He chewed his cigar over that and said, "My wife's name is Ethel."

"Do you know Lucy McDermott? Or maybe you're related to her," I suggested.

"No." He uprooted himself and closed the door in my face.

I made a firm decision to try a different approach with George, who lived on (you might know) Myra Street a couple of miles to the east of Milton.

Myra Street was a combination of the old and the new. The house I was looking for was of the latter, a low-slung ranch-type affair with a picture window and horseshoe drive. They were still working on the sidewalks in front of it. I parked and jumped across the moist, dug-up earth and went up the drive to the door. Another screen separated me from George, a tall thin man with nervous eyes, one long eyebrow above them, a beak of a nose, and a gaunt face.

"Mr. George McDermott?"

"Who's askin'?" It was a shallow voice that clipped the words out. Not at all the kind of voice you'd have expected to come out from underneath that nose.

"The name is Rafferty. I'm a private investigator from New Orleans."

"That so," he said like he was real interested.

"I'm trying to locate a woman named Lucy McDermott. Ever heard of her?"

He paused longer than he should have had to. "No, can't say that I have," he said, "but I tell you what. You hang on right there and I'll go get my wife. She's always gettin' together with the womenfolk around here and she just might know. You hang on."

He made sure the screened door was locked, closed the

door behind it and locked it, too, and I hung on. I should
have known better but the idea to bolt didn't get strong until I had smoked a cigarette halfway down. I ground it out
and was leaving when I heard the lock being turned.
George McDermott shoved a pudgy woman, who kept running her tongue across her top lip, ahead of him to the door.
She coughed discreetly and swiveled her head to glance up
and back at him and got a prod in the back for bothering.

"I never heard of a Lucy McDermott," she blurted, her
voice raising an octave on the first syllable of Lucy.

"You sure now, honey?" The words were crawling from
George's mouth now. "This man's come all the way from
New Orleans to find her, so it must be important." His eyes
darted from the street to me and back again.

The woman didn't answer. She didn't have to—George
had stalled long enough. A black and white job with a cherry on top turned into the horseshoe. Two men in khaki uni-
forms alighted lethargically from the car, one of them
resting his hand on his gun butt.

"This here's the man, Earl," George clipped self-
importantly.

"Well, now, you done right to call me, George." Earl
turned his receding sandy curls to me. He still had on sunglasses although the sun had long since started slipping its
way into the west. "Looks as if you and me are going to get
the opportunity to know each other, mister," he drawled. I
thought grimly of going through the Big City P.I. Has Showdown With Small Town Law Enforcement Official routine.
"Give him a go over, Shark."

Shark had a face that could have stopped a train. His nose
was so bent it looked like it was trying to get in his right eye,
one cheek was going to be blue and puffed and a little higher than the other one forever. I could have fit my kitchen
table in his mouth and used his top lip for a tablecloth. But
Shark knew his business. He lumbered over with his right
hand still on his gun butt and with his powerful left twisted

my right arm behind me and shoved me over to the car, thereby indicating that I should assume a position against the car amenable to search. I did. He poked, prodded, slapped, scraped me down and swiftly extracted my gun.

"Thought you'd want to know, Earl," George was saying behind me.

"Sure thing. I always want to know when we got a visitor." Shark turned me around so I could see him niftily slide my gun through the air where it thudded neatly in Earl's hand. "Well, now, mister," Earl said as he inspected the machinery, "I think we oughta let the McDermotts here get back to their peaceful home life while you and me have a nice informative chat back at the department." His deputy's badge glinted in the light over the door.

"That's too bad, George," I imitated Earl's drawl and threw some disappointment around the edges. George's one eyebrow shot up involuntarily. "That you won't get to watch me bite the deputy on the hand."

Earl gave a derisive laugh as the door whooshed back into its frame, but Shark didn't like my sense of humor. "Watch that business," he muttered threateningly through his thick lips and pushed me down into the back seat. The doors locked me behind a strong mesh screen. Shark climbed in front with Earl.

"You sure you wouldn't feel safer if I was wearing handcuffs?" I asked, but no one answered. I wouldn't exist until we were in the sheriff's office.

30

The Dead Aunt

EARL SLAPPED a straight-backed chair on the side of his desk and eased himself on top of a frayed cushion in the seat of a wooden swivel chair behind it. Six pairs of eyes watched every move. The only person in the big room who was uninterested was Shark. He busied himself with the loose papers lying all over his desk. Earl carefully removed his sunglasses and rested them on top of a plastic pen holder. A finger darted under a stack of paper, bending the edges back so he could sneak a look at whatever was underneath. He diddled around some more so that he could build up the suspense that was already killing me. When I could stand it no more, he leaned back, folded his hands over his stomach, and gave me his undivided attention.

"State your name and your business," he said efficiently. I did. "You got an identifying card?" He leaned forward, extending his index and third fingers. I took out my wallet and showed him. He looked at it a long time, then turned it over and looked at it some more. I got a hard stare as he handed it back. He examined me almost as minutely as he had the card. I held my eyes open for inspection and remembered not to sigh too audibly. This Earl was tough, no two ways about it. He set his face into a plastic smile.

"Now you know, Rafferty, most gun-carrying strangers who come to our town here remember to drop by and give us a howdy-do. I guess it slipped your mind, though." He was being so polite I wished I had a raw beefsteak to shove down his throat.

"No, it didn't slip my mind," I said. The smile started slipping out of the corners of his mouth. "I didn't know it was a town custom."

He tightened the smile into a grimace. "Well, now you know." He picked up a ball-point pen and clicked it slowly a couple of times. "Just what business you got in our neck of the woods?"

"I'm sure George was happy to fill you in on that."

The pen clicked to writing position and he shoved the point into the stack of papers. "I want to hear it from you," he said, not quite yelling. The paper shuffling around the room slackened and stopped. The only sound was the slow click of the pen as Earl's big thumb mashed the button. Furtive eyes darted conspicuously and ears flapped in the breeze. Earl swept the room through slits and the paper moving resumed. Things must have been slack in Santa Rosa.

"Okay," I said. "I guess George was too excited to get it straight." His big thumb came down so hard on the pen that his nail turned white. "I'm trying to locate a woman named Lucy McDermott for questioning in connection with the murder of her employer in New Orleans. I understand she spent time in the neighborhood of Gulf Breeze. Could be she has relatives in the area that she might be staying with, so here I am."

He stared at me with a face devoid of comprehension, or any expression for that matter. "Hey, Shark. Where've I heard the name Lucy McDermott before?"

Shark swiveled his chair languidly. "We got an APB on her." Shark was one of those types who always mutters threateningly no matter what he is saying, only he could adjust the mutter to carry over a mountaintop.

"Don't tell me," I said to Earl. "You knew it all along."

His neck jutted, pushing his face halfway across the desk. "Now you look here Mr. Wise Guy. We gonna get somethin' straight and we gonna get it straight right now. This here, right here," he slapped the desk, "is the law in this town. When the sheriff ain't here, I'm in charge. You got business here, you come and speak it to me or the sheriff. Now that's the first thing you ought to remember. The second thing is we don't like strangers like you showing up on the doorstep of our private citizens askin' a lot of questions. We ask the questions around here and people like George McDermott know that and like it. Now if you don't like it we got ways of makin' you like it. The fact of the matter is that we got our own ways of doin' just about everything. And that's why we got law and order in this county and people that like law and order." He sat back like he'd just made the acceptance speech for the Nobel Peace Prize.

"I can see that you keep your boys busy and in shape, though." He either didn't get it or let it pass. He just sat there looking like he didn't understand anything, which I decided was his way of being tough. "Look, Deputy, I wasn't trying to cut you boys out of the action. For all I know there won't be any. I may be in the wrong part of Florida. The woman may have come from Miami and just liked to visit the beach areas around here. All I know is she had an aunt who died and who she was close to and that she liked Gulf Breeze. So I thought I'd take a trip down here and check out the records for inheritances over the past couple of months. Maybe the aunt owned a house around here and left it to the McDermott woman. Only trouble is I got here a little too late to do much checking. Sure, it's a shot in the dark, but what does anyone have to go on? The woman's holed up somewhere and this is as good a place to start looking as any."

"What makes you think you're more efficient than the New Orleans Police Department?" he asked.

"Nothing. I just like to finish what I start. Detective Lieutenant Roderick Rankin knows I'm working on this case. You can check that out with a phone call."

More blank stare and then: "And just how did you get started on this case?"

"I found the body." He didn't seem moved. "Go ahead, check it out," I said gesturing at the phone.

Apparently I wasn't going to rate high on the popularity polls no matter what. Saying nothing, Earl got up and strolled over to Shark's desk where something like a pow-wow went on. He came back and shoved a blank piece of paper in front of me and clicked the ball point open. Handing me the pen he said, "Write Rankin's number and yours underneath." I put them down and passed the paper to him. He picked up the phone and leaned back, cradling the receiver in his neck.

"This here's Dep'ty Slade," he said after a moment. "I want to make a person-to-person call to Detective Lieutenant Rankin." He reeled off the number. There was a pause. "Now hold on a minute, sweetheart. I want you to charge that call to another number." He glanced at me with something like amusement and then he gave my office number to the operator. I made a gesture of helplessness that was the first thing I'd done since I'd been there that was appreciated. After a longer pause and a lot of clicking coming from both the phone and the pen, Earl straightened up in the chair, put the pen down, and held on tight to the receiver. With an ingratiating smile widening his mouth, he spoke.

"Lieutenant Rankin, this's Dep'ty Earl Slade, Santa Rosa County, Florida. We got a dick here says he's Neal Rafferty. Says he's working with you on the Stanley Garber murder. You know him? I see," Earl said. Uncle Roddy was probably setting him straight about how close we were working together. Earl handed the phone to me with three fingers over the mouthpiece. "He wants to talk to you," he said.

I took the phone. "Greetings, Lieutenant."

"What the hell are you doing now, Neal?" he bellowed.

"Well, there hasn't been much action, Lieutenant. Just thought I'd do some checking on Lucy McDermott's dead aunt." I smiled nicely at Earl.

"What dead aunt?" he shrieked. I'd never heard him so excited.

"Yes, Lieutenant, I was sure Catherine Garber had mentioned to you that Lucy McDermott left town a couple of months back to attend her aunt's funeral," I said, intimating that Uncle Roddy knew exactly what I was talking about.

"Nobody mentioned nothin' of the kind to me." I didn't say anything. He went on. "Nobody tells the cops nothin'. We don't have time to get cozy with all the principals in a case," he said. "Did she say the aunt died in Florida?"

"No."

"Well, then, what the hell are you doing there? We *got* an APB out."

"So I heard. Anyway, that could take a long time if she's holed up waiting for the heat to subside. I thought the aunt might go along with that passion for Florida I told you about. Maybe she left Lucy a house or something."

He sighed. "It's your time, Neal."

"Sure thing, Lieutenant," I said pleasantly, and handed the phone back to Earl.

Earl laughed into the mouthpiece. "You boys got so much work you gotta hire private dicks?" The smile vanished. "Yes, sir," he said seriously, "we can do that." Uncle Roddy was still excited. I couldn't understand what he was saying, but I could hear his voice buzzing. "We'll get right on it," Earl said and dropped the phone back on the hook. I got a steady, efficient gaze. "How long ago did that aunt die?"

"That's not certain. You might have to all the way back to the first of the year." I stood up. "It's not certain the aunt's name was McDermott either."

Earl looked disgusted. "You better know damn well what

you're talking about, Rafferty. I'm gonna have to pull one of those records boys away from dinner and a nice night at home to do this. You just better know what you're talking about."

"I already told you it's a shot in the dark."

"A shot in the dark worth more than a couple of hours of work," he said glumly. I've never figured yet why it takes the bureaucrats twice as much time as it would take a grammar school kid to do the same thing.

"It'll be appreciated," I said.

"Not if we don't find anything, it won't."

"I'll appreciate it anyway," I told him. He leered at me. "By the way, do you mind if I take my hardware back now?"

"You'll get it back when you leave town," he snarled.

I could have told him that was unconstitutional and done a lot of squawking. But he was doing the favors so I told him I'd check back with him in a couple of hours instead. Also, I was foolish enough to think I wouldn't need a gun.

His hand was moving toward the telephone as I left.

31

The Bartender

SHARK DROVE ME BACK to my car, which was still parked across the street from George McDermott's house. I was in no mood for light conversation, so it didn't particularly bother me that he was being antisocial. He drove the car like he was sitting in an easy chair, one hand loosely attached to the top of the steering wheel and an elbow hanging out of the window. His eyes never deviated from the road even when he stopped beside my car. Never having had anything against being polite, I thanked him for the ride. His head turned like it was on a stick, the muscles in his jaw flexed, and he showed me the finest in a whole line of contempt. He watched me while I got in the car and then he did a U-turn in George's driveway and followed me down the street. And he kept following me. I didn't know where I was going, but it wasn't in the direction we had come from. I made a few unnecessary turns and even went around a block just for the hell of it, and there he was—right behind me the whole time. He didn't even make an effort to pretend he wasn't there. I drove in a straight line for a while and then on a whim made a right. When I straightened out I noticed with surprise that there were no headlights in the rearview mirror. An eighth of a mile later I found out why. I

was on a dead-end street. After a difficult turnaround, I
headed back to the adjacent avenue. He had pulled up to
the curb and was waiting for me. I turned and pulled to the
side of the street and got out of the car and walked back to
where he was sitting. He had the same look of contempt
plastered on his dumb features. I nonchalantly put my forearm on the top of the car and assumed a stance.

"Shark," I said, "I'm going to tell you exactly what I'm going to do in case we get separated. There's a little seafood
restaurant at the end of Santa Rosa Island next to the Na-
varre Beach Motel. I'm going to have dinner there and then
I'm going to find a bar and have a few drinks. It's been a
lousy few days and I need them. After that I figure I should
have killed enough time that I can head back to Milton and
see what the records man has come up with. What I do after
that depends on what he's got. I'll invite you to dinner, but
only with the understanding that we go dutch. The same
with the drinks if you don't think Deputy Slade will mind
that you have a few in the line of duty. How does that sound
to you?"

"Up yours, dick," he snarled.

"I'm open for suggestions, but that wasn't exactly what I
had in mind."

"That's tough," he said and spit with perfect aim so that
the wad landed right in front of my left shoe.

"Personality and good looks," I said, stepping back from
the wet spot. "You must really charm 'em all."

I walked away from him and back to my car. There wasn't
a peep out of him. He must have expended his entire vo-
cabulary. I decided that the evening I had outlined to him
sounded okay, and I tried to put it out of my mind that I had
acquired a second shadow while in Milton. The Escambia
McDermott's would have to wait until the next day unless
Shark decided that I was harmless after all.

I thought about the past four days and where they had got

me. Something felt wrong. I reviewed the case as I saw it. First, hot-stuff detective is hired by hot-stuff man-about-town to find the missing rare, expensive books. High intrigue. Hot-stuff detective finds a body first. Promising. Only to find out that the man's son took the books. So the detective gets paid a nice fat fee for kicking around in the family dirt. At least he finds out, though, that he isn't the only one who has problems with his old man. But he can't forget about the body, so he kicks around in a few more families' dirt, meets some fascinating people, and gets told a few sheltered facts. Once again it looks promising, but where does it all lead? To a wild goose chase in Florida, which would have been okay if it had remained his own private wild goose chase. Instead it becomes the business of the New Orleans Police Department, his Uncle Roddy, and a hostile deputy who doesn't like to work and who sics a shadow on him that would make Buster Brown look like a beauty queen. And the deputy is probably going to get downright nasty when he finds out that he did a few finger exercises on the telephone for nothing.

Shark didn't quite tailgate me all the way to the restaurant. I went up the paved area between two expanses of sand to the front of the place. He parked across the road unobtrusively and cut his lights. I couldn't tell if he had cut the motor because of the pounding of the surf. I took a seat by a window facing the water so I wouldn't have to look at his mug if he decided to come in. I ordered beer and a large seafood platter and spent a lot of time over it all. But Shark wasn't likely to get discouraged; his type isn't familiar with impatience.

That's why it turned me around a bit when I went out and discovered that he was gone. I strolled down the beach in the darkness and breathed in the salty air and tossed a few memories around, all the while expecting to see the car sandwiched in between a couple of dunes. It wasn't and it didn't pop out behind me as I drove down the road to the other end of the island. I started breathing easier but I still wasn't sure.

There is only one main highway on the narrow island called Santa Rosa, and it runs parallel with the Gulf of Mexico only a couple of hundred yards from it. Sand dunes dot both sides of the road and every once in a while light from a beach house will wink at you from among the dunes. The scarce street lights are saved for prominent corners in the tiny web of sandy, lettered avenues.

I had been the only car on the road for a long while, but as I neared the end of the island where a bridge connects it to Gulf Breeze there was more activity. Then the lights from the small shopping center and group of stores, gas stations, restaurants, and bars all built near the public beach loomed ahead. As I approached the noise got louder and the activity increased. This part of Santa Rosa is where the college set congregates during the summer. They yell to each other above a din created by the sounds of rock music and revving engines. I got stuck in a pint-sized traffic jam caused by a stalled car. The guy behind pushed the car out of the parking lot in front of the bar while a line of horn honkers eagerly waited for their empty spaces. I waited too, having decided that, to be on the safe side, I'd go have a few drinks instead of bounding over to Escambia.

The guy in the stalled car finally managed to peel out, which is apparently the only acceptable way to leave the parking lot. I spotted a place across the street on the side of a restaurant and parked there instead of spending the rest of the night trying to get a slot in front of the bar. I was in definite need of a drink by the time I waded through the contest of who could look best coming and going.

The inside of the bar was typical: small, smoky, crowded, and noisy. There was the usual absence of enough tables and bar stools, but plenty of posters set at weird angles of the ever-current favorites, like James Dean and Marlon Brando.

Brando appeared twice—on a motorcycle and with his heavy jowls. Standing around the bar in the front were tight-jeaned guys and giggling girls who looked like they had spent their lives on the beach and could stand up forever. As I made my way through them, getting a few snickers for my suit, a roar went up in the back where the game tables were grouped and a big bruiser lifted a Foosball table above his head and shook it. He'd probably been doing that to the waves all day. When he dropped it back down to the floor, the building shook and a cry sounded for more beer. The atypical bartender in a white apron and with all forty-five years or so showing on his face started sliding pitchers of the stuff down to the end of the bar nearest the games. I went down to a lone stool against the wall.

The bartender came wringing his hands on his apron. He wiped off the scarred piece of wood in front of me.

"You must mix a mean brew," I said.

"Ha!" He flourished the cloth. "I got—how do they call it?—charisma." He leaned one arm on the bar and took me in. "And you. You must need a drink bad or you just escaped from a loony bin." He surveyed the room.

"And *you*?" I countered.

"I ain't here for my health—I own the joint. What'll it be?"

I ordered bourbon, since it was hard to find these days in New Orleans. While he poured it a guy with enormous biceps banged on the bar for attention. "Hey, Al, we need a pitcher down here. We're thirsty," he explained. The group around him gave a raucous laugh in appreciation of his little joke.

The bartender tossed his head. "In a minute, Harry—if you can hold on to your DTs that long." Everyone within hearing laughed at that. I could see what Al meant about his having charisma.

He put my bourbon in front of me. "The name of the game is tolerance, who can drink the most," he said as he picked my money up. "They're in here proving their man-hood."

"It must be good for business."

"That's the other reason I'm here." He picked up a pitch-er and drew beer into it, not bothering to cut the clouds. Harry and his gang were past the point of noticing things like that.

Al came back to the sink underneath me and started washing pitchers on a couple of brushes sticking up out of sudsy water.

"Is it like this every night?" I asked.

"Only in the summer and never on Sundays, thank God."

"Ever thought about getting some help?"

"You applying for the job?" He snorted a laugh. "Naw, they'll rob you blind. Couple of summers back I hired this nice young guy spending the summer down here from Har-vard. Clean cut; none of this bearded weirdo stuff. Funny thing, though, the take got cut almost in half the first two weeks he's here. Harvard tells me business is slow. This I find hard to believe, so I says to this friend of mine, I says, 'Look, I'll front you and you go spend a couple of nights down at the bar and tell me what goes.' So he does. Mean-while, I lie low. See? Anyway, I talk to my friend a few nights later and he says business looks good to him. I can't figure it. I tell him to spend a couple more nights, just to make sure, but he says the same. I'm baffled but I figure Harvard's on the take and somehow my friend just ain't catching him stashing the stuff. So, much as I'm under the weather that year and it's a twenty-mile drive from my house to here, I decide I better drop in on Harvard. You know, a little surprise. I tell my friend the plan of attack over a game of gin rummy and he says it sounds like a good plan to him. Then he says, 'By the way, Al, where'd you get that fancy new cash register?'

" 'What fancy new cash register?' I says. 'That's the same cash register that's always been there.'

" 'Naw,' he says, 'I mean the antique job with the carved inlays.'

"Well, there ain't no antique job with the carved inlays. Get the picture? Harvard brought his own cash register. It was one for him and one for me."

"Well, they say you've got to have brains to get into Harvard." I thought about my first case. One of Maurice's clients, a bar owner, had a bartender who brought his own bottles.

"Yeah. And this guy's in the law school yet." I laughed. "If that kind of stuff don't tell you why this country's going to pot. . . . You ready for another one?"

I was ready and so was everyone else in the joint. Al slapped another bourbon in front of me and then slaved over the tap for a while. Then he was back to the sink and the dirty glasses with a sigh. It wasn't necessary with a dish drainer on the side, but he polished glass briskly with a towel as if he had to keep his hands busy. "What parts you from?" he asked. His manner of speaking was as clipped as his rubbing was brisk. I told him. "That's a ways to come to have a drink in this dump. And you don't look like the fun-in-the-sun type."

"True. You might say I was on a little business, but the lady doesn't seem to be around."

A contemptuous laugh. "Women," he said. "You might as well of been out in the sun for three days straight if you got one of 'em on your mind. You got to be with 'em every second or they run off with the first thing that shows up in a pair of pants. Then if you bother to catch up with 'em, they pull hysterics on you about how they can't stand to be alone. Don't think I don't know, what with being in the bar business all these years and having my nights taken up. They come in and they all got eyes for the bartender. You make eyes back at one and two days later she's telling you that you don't spend enough time with her. Hell, she knew what business you were in. I guess that's why I stick with this joint. At least you don't get that brand of trouble with the teeny-bops. Anyway, you got my sympathies, bud."

"Maybe it isn't quite like that."

He peered at me through the dimness. "If you say so. I've kidded myself before, too." I didn't say anything. "Hell, maybe I'm being a sourpuss." That still got him nothing. "Or maybe you mean what you say—you got business."

I twirled my empty glass around and he brought the bottle over and set it down. I poured myself another drink and he resumed his glass polishing.

"Well, Al," I shrugged, "who's to say if I say what I mean or not." I looked resigned and got some more sympathy. "Say, Al," I said with sudden hopefulness, "maybe you know the lady."

"Could be, if she's ever made the mistake of wandering in here. Of course, during the winter I get an older crowd. What's her name?"

"Lucy McDermott."

"No, I don't know her," he said slowly. I felt my gut tighten. And it wasn't pure instinct. It was the absence of his clipped tone, the way his toweling hand slowed down, the way he put the glass very gingerly on the counter, the way he picked up the bottle of bourbon and the money and moved off. I sipped on my drink, watching his every move. He never turned around even when I tried to get his attention to order another drink. I've made wrong guesses, but I think he wanted me gone. It was too bad: He couldn't go anywhere and I was right where I wanted to be. I sat tight and waited. The crowd would be thinning out to nothing and then we would be alone together. Blissfully alone. I just wished he'd left the bottle of bourbon; it was going to be a long wait without it.

32

Lights Out

I SPENT THE BETTER PART of an hour in the wings viewing Al's backside and marvelous profile and that's about all the time there was before curtain call.

The air had gotten thicker and the crowd noisier and one of Al's beer taps had gone dry. Behind me the Foosball table was being tossed, pounded, and turned on its side, and the big bruiser who looked like he had just walked off the set of *Muscle Beach Party* and was doing the maneuvering had run through several sets of challengers and emerged the still unbeaten champ. I was fast slipping over the edge into headachy moroseness.

All it took was one time, just one time out of the forty a minute that the door opened and banged shut. A big guy with something peculiar about his looks came in. It was the tiny half-inch bangs over his big, heavy face. A piranha nipping at my rear end couldn't have lifted it off the stool faster than the sight of the Boy Scout did. He moved through the crowd like Moses through the Red Sea and shoved his flabby torso sausaged into a Ban-Lon shirt against the other end of the bar. I moved off so he wouldn't see me and felt about as inconspicuous as a hunchback at a garden party, but he hadn't seen me yet. Al hurried over to him and they conferred, leaning low across the bar. I scrunched down, trying to use a buck-toothed youth half as wide as myself as camouflage, but the Boy Scout's fringed head bobbed up and his eyes locked on me like I was the only other animal in the cage. Al reached for an unopened bottle, and Groz began to quickly slap bills on the counter. That was my cue. I pushed through the bodies, passed a lot of Pepsodent smiles in tanned faces, waved to Al, who stood rigidly behind the bar, and a year later opened the door and choked on the clean, salty air.

The Boy Scout had vanished. I looked for him in every direction and in his tight red Ban-Lon he should have been about as hard to spot as Diamond Jim in a fish tank. I went down to the end of the row of buildings where there was a grassy lot. I peered between the parked cars for a crouching hulk. I crossed over to the other end of the buildings where there was another weedy alley and went along the side of a building, which housed a combination sporting goods store and drugstore, to the highway. On the other side of the glassed displays of aspirin, sunglasses, baseball hats and beach paraphernalia a street intersected the highway. There were only so many places to go. The most accessible escape routes were down the street, into the hamburger joint on the other side, or into the restaurant I'd parked the car next to. I hesitated to leave the street, knowing that if I chose the wrong place I could lose him forever so I walked slowly in front of the drug-sporting store to the corner, shoved my hands in my pockets, and consoled myself with the thought that there was still Al.

I stood at the corner for a few moments where I had a good view of the highway in both directions. Nothing. The side street became covered in darkness after half a block so I walked down the concrete edge to get a better look and was just about even with the back of the hamburger place when I heard a car engine accelerate behind it. A red sportster darted into the street, its headlights aimed at me. And it kept coming. I jumped into the weedy sand and as I hit the ground the car went over the edge as the driver tried to straighten out. Rubber scraped and the car jumped back into the street. There was more revving while Groz turned his fat head to me and gave me what I can only describe as an invitational smirk. Then he ground the gears, squealed all the way to the corner, and turned smartly onto the highway just in time to cut off another car which jerked to a stop.

I raced to the corner, crossed the highway, and jumped into my car. By the time I bypassed the main activity, the only things in sight were two taillights far down the road. My efforts to catch up with them were futile and about ten minutes later they turned to the left down one of the lettered avenues. I was too far away to judge the distance accurately, but I wasn't worried that Groz was trying to give me the slip. His smirk had been a definite dare to follow, and I had a hunch he was as ready for a showdown as I was.

I turned where I thought he had and drove down the half-lit street. Houses in this area were sparse and some of them looked like they had already been closed down for the summer. I tooled slowly around the blocks looking for the red car and hung a left to get back on the first street running parallel with the highway. A couple of blocks down a car was pulled up on the curb in front of a house. I drove toward it. It was Groz's car. I passed it and parked on the opposite side of the street a block away. I could feel him waiting for me and without a gun it was a nasty feeling so I opted for the sneak approach around the back of the house.

There were no lights on in the house and the street light was too far away to penetrate the darkness. I wondered if he was playing games and had parked in front of the wrong house deliberately, but a tension told me to keep going.

I went around the back of the only other house on the block, a couple of hundred feet away from the house I was trying to get to. The sneak approach would be impossible—

the only cover between where I stood and the house were the shadows I was already standing in. Not even a measly dune was in sight. I was walking into an obvious trap and I silently cursed Earl Slade for keeping my gun.

About the only thing I had left to use was pure bluff. I went back to the street and walked down the sidewalk to the house with my fist bunched up in my coat pocket. My legs didn't like the idea much and felt stiff and awkward, but somehow I ended up in front of the house in one piece. I felt better for a moment but the creepy feeling came back when nothing happened. I took a deep breath and walked boldly to the front door and knocked. When that didn't work, I went around to the side of the house and walked through the open carport, my hand still in my pocket. At the back of the house was a screened porch. I walked around it to the other side. The last window before the porch was shut but not draped. I peered inside and what I saw made me jump: the outline of a woman sitting in the middle of a sofa facing the front door. I cupped my hands around my face to make sure I wasn't seeing things. She sat with her back to me, perfectly still.

I knocked on the glass. "Miss McDermott," I called. I thought I saw her shoulders twitch almost imperceptibly, but she didn't turn around or move otherwise. I started rattling the glass again and calling to her and was so intent on getting her to turn to me that I wasn't aware that anyone was behind me until it was too late.

A flash of white light was the last thing I saw.

33

One Way to Convince Louie

I CAME AROUND to a lot of shouting and a woman crying. The backs of my eyelids felt like they were jammed with sticks. I kept them shut and laid still and tried to concentrate on what was being said instead of the nausea and a headache that was coming on fast.

"You want ole Louie to put your lights out for good, you just keep on with your goddamn lies." I recognized the slightly nasal tenor as Groz's. "You told Al not to tell anyone where you were. That was me you were talkin' about." The woman let out a gasped sob as something thudded on wood. "Stop that goddamn crying and give out with some answers. Shit. I didn't come all the way down here to listen to your bleating."

The sobs subsided a bit. "I swear, Louie, I never laid eyes on him before. I don't know him. You gotta believe that. I swear, I'm not lying."

"Screw that. I might of believed you if he hadn't shown up here. You expect me to believe that he just happened to show up right here on this fuckin' island by accident? To your little hideaway that you were always so careful about keeping a secret?" He laughed. "I just bet, baby, that you didn't even think old Louie would remember, did you?" He paused and then yelled it again. "Did you, goddammit?"

"No, Louie," she said quickly. "You got it all wrong. I figured you'd remember. I had to get out quick. I couldn't stick around to wait for you. I been waiting for you here. I knew you'd remember."

"So you said. Only I don't see it that way. The way I got it figured is you were trying to cut me out of my dues and I don't like that."

"No, Louie," she said miserably. "That's not so. I told you already—I didn't get any more money out of Stan. I couldn't. He threatened to blow the whistle so I had to get out."

"Funny how he never threatened that before. Funny how it all happens the minute I leave town. It even gets funnier when you think about how the day I get back I find this goddamn punk in the apartment." His heels clicked on the hard floor as he moved in the direction of her voice. I moved one eyelid a fraction. I could see his hair clipped short all over his skull. "You know what I think, Lucy? I think he got my part of the dough and it was him you were waiting for."

He was standing in front of her, blocking her from my view. "You're crazy, Louie," she said in a resigned voice.

"I'm crazy, am I?" He raised his arm and slapped her hard. She broke into renewed sobs. "You bitch. Don't you ever tell me I'm crazy." He walked away from her over to a sideboard where a bottle of bourbon and glasses stood. Lucy had her face buried in her arms, leaning over the side of a shabby chair. Thick dark auburn hair cascaded from her head onto her shoulders. I hoisted myself up on an elbow. A gun appeared like magic in the Boy Scout's hand.

"You take it slow and easy, punk." The gun jerked nervously toward me, but he didn't seem to be drunk and that worried me. I had been lying on a thin Indian rug covering a cold concrete floor in front of the sofa. I got up slowly, testing the back of my head to see if it was still there. Louie's eyes were glittering brown holes in the puffed, flabby flesh around them. They twitched in their sockets. "Sit down there and don't move a fuckin' inch or you're dead," he said indicating the sofa. I did as I was told. The nervous eyes seemed to control his gun hand. Everytime they darted, the gun jerked. The palms of my hands began to sweat like they tend to do when a lunatic has a nervous gun aimed at you. For his kind it's easier to pull the trigger than not to. I sat very still, watching him as his eyeballs jumped from me to Lucy.

Her cries stopped. The only sound in the room was the chair creaking as she sat up in it. Her wavy hair dripped into her eyes and she pushed it back with crimson fingertips. Her face was swollen from crying and even under what looked like three layers of stage makeup I could see a bruise on her jaw. Where Louie's fingers had contacted her cheek purplish lines were starting to show under the rouge. Her eyebrows were rather bushy and black and underneath them were great big green eyes with thick false eyelashes that rose up to cuddle her forehead. Mascara coursed down her face. All she needed was a baggy suit and shoes three sizes too large to make the saddest of sad clowns. But her bone structure was fine, the eyes beautiful. Her face seemed relatively unlined, although who could tell under all that powder. If the hair was dyed, it was a good job. She could have been a handsome woman without the goo and the misery.

Louie's mouth curled into a sinister smile. "Looks like we have a little reunion here," he snarled.

"I tell you, Louie, I never saw him before," Lucy whined.

"The lady is telling the truth, Louie," I chimed in.

"Who asked you, punk?" He opened the bottle of bourbon and poured three fingers neat. I remembered what Murphy said and felt better as he drained the glass.

"I just thought I'd try to clarify matters."

He poured himself another drink. "We'll get to that. Where's the dough?" The gun jumped at me.

"If you're talking about blackmail money from Stanley Garber, I wouldn't know."

He slammed the glass on the sideboard. "Get off that line, asshole." He advanced toward me with the gun pointed at my nose. "I know all about you. You're nothin' but a shit-eatin' dick living cheap." His eyes were beginning to take on a alcoholic shine. "I seen your set up. You'd jump out of ten feet of water for some dough. All you got is your cheap good looks. You're the kind makes suckers out of broads. I seen millions like you, punk. You get a woman like Lucy here and before she knows what the fuck happened, you got her goin' halvseys with you. Don't think I ain't seen it before. How many you got pumpin' it to you, asshole?"

He swaggered, gave a sniveling laugh, and turned to Lucy. The gun was still on me. "You shoulda seen the piece of class that came calling on him last night, baby. It would have made you eat your heart out." He looked back at me. "That dame saved your life, you punk. I would have killed you. I would have killed you!" he yelled. His lower lip came out and he stood there quaking like a child throwing a temper tantrum who had long since forgotten why. On his flabby face under the fringe of hair was that curious combination of incomprehension and stubborness. It didn't take a mastermind to figure out that Lucy and I didn't know each other. He was acting like he had missed a few cards when the deck had been passed out. Fear slipped into Lucy's face until it looked on the verge of being torn apart with fright. I guessed that she was quite familiar with the violence behind the childlike temper, violence that could be triggered as easily as the gun he was holding. I didn't like the way he was trembling. It made me a dead man too easily.

"Look, Louie," I said, "if you hadn't been so busy shooting

at me, tearing up my place, and trying to scare me to death, we might have gotten this straightened out last night. Lucy and I don't know each other."

"Bullshit," he said. He looked at me with hatred. I think he knew Lucy wanted to dump him, and in his mind that meant there was another man. "I shoulda burned Curly's down when you were inside. It would have saved me a lot of trouble."

Holy shit, I thought. Murphy is going to want to do a slow torture on this guy. "Louie, you saw me follow you out here tonight to find this place. Why would I do that if I knew Lucy? If Lucy was waiting here for me? And what about Al giving me the fish eye back in the bar? I'm on this island partially by luck and partially because I've been looking for Lucy since I found Garber's body Monday. It's taken me that long to put it all together. Think about it. Maybe she's telling you the truth about having to get out. The police are looking for her because they think she plugged Garber. Once they start asking a lot of questions, the whole black-mail scheme is going to come out. They're going to want to know what all of those little gift bonuses were for. That wouldn't be good for Lucy or for you. Maybe she thought the best way would be to hole up until some of the heat let up. She couldn't very well tell you where she'd be if you were out of town. Think about it."

A shaky left hand wiped the beads of sweat from his up-per lip. "Yeah? The old lady told me she left Sunday and the paper said Garber was killed Monday." He said it like that clarified the matter, but he looked confused. He stumbled backward to the sideboard and poured a drink. With the gun trained slightly above my head he gulped it down and took a handkerchief from a back pocket and wiped the back of his neck. The liquor had helped his shakes some so he poured another one and gulped it and then stood leaning like an old sock the dog had been chewing on. His brain was having a hard time assimilating.

"Maybe it wasn't me you were talkin' to Al about. If you don't know him," he waved the gun at me, "and it wasn't me you were hiding from . . ." He began to pace in front of the sofa, his eyes darting from me to Lucy in the chair at the side.

"Move over there," he commanded Lucy, waving the gun at the sofa. She got up and sat close to the arm. Now it was easier for him to watch both of us. Something was forming in his mass of gray and he didn't want his concentration spoiled by having to watch two places at once. He went back and leaned on the sideboard, but wired now, not limp.

"I get it, you bitch," he said. "Let's hear how it happened."

"What, Louie?" she asked, her hands fidgeting nervously with the long tie belt drawing in the waist of the black dress she was wearing.

"How you killed him," he hissed through his teeth.

Her mouth dropped open and then she managed a laugh. "Me? Me kill Stan? Why?"

"I thought you said he wouldn't cough up," he sneered.

"That's right, but I didn't kill him. I never even saw him after Saturday." He just stood there sneering, working himself into another fit. "I'll tell you what happened, Louie, but it's not what you're thinking." She chattered nervously. "I had to get out—it all happened so fast I didn't know what to do. And you were gone, Louie. Who did I have to turn to?" Coyness started displacing the nervousness. She was working on him the way she knew best. "That Sunday, after you left, I stayed around the apartment. There was a knock on the door—it was Mrs. Garber pointing a gun at me. It's not like I had any choice about letting her in. She was standing there with that gun on me and telling me she knew all about the money Stan had been giving me. And then—I swear, Louie, you're not gonna believe this," she laughed, "she tells me she's gonna kill me because I been having an affair with Stan. I swear, Louie, she meant it—she was gonna kill me.

So I did the only thing I knew to do. I told her it wasn't an affair but that I'd been blackmailing him because I knew he had another daughter. She laughed at that and said she already knew that, so why the blackmail. So I said, 'Maybe you know, but your daughter doesn't.' Well, that gave her something to think about, Louie. She told me she'd let me go, but that I better get out of town fast or she'd kill me.''

"You stupid bitch ..." Louie started, but she broke him off.

"Wait a minute, Louie, that isn't all. She left after she saw I started packing. As soon as she got out the door practically, I called Stan and told him I wanted ten grand for getting out and not causing any trouble. I tell you, Louie, it floored me when he said no. I figured he didn't have it, but I played it right. I swear, I did. I told him he had to get it and I'd give him a day and that's when he said I better get out or he would blow. What was I supposed to do? I mean, with that crazy wife of his running around with guns and stuff. I thought I better get out and wait for you to handle it. That's the way it happened, Louie, I swear." She took a deep breath.

Louie thought that over for a while. "No," he said finally, "no, that don't add."

"What do you mean?"

"Since when were you afraid of a little old lady?" he asked. "What do you think old Louie is? A half-wit? Is that what you think? You don't remember telling me about Garber sayin' his wife was getting on to the money and thought he was makin' it with you? You don't remember that, do you baby? That was a long time ago. She's gonna come around with a gun now?" He was yelling again.

Lucy's hand jerked at the belt. "Uh-uh, Louie, you got it wrong," she said cautiously. "Stan said she *might* start thinking that."

"Shit. She's gonna kill you because you're having an affair with him but she's gonna let you go 'cause you're blackmailing him? Let me tell you what happened. Mrs. Garber never showed up. You decided that it was a good time to give old Louie the slip. So you moved out of the apartment and holed up somewhere else, maybe with him"—he motioned at me—"maybe with that son of a bitch André. And then you went to work Monday morning and told Garber you wanted the money right now. You couldn't wait for me so we could do it like we planned. You were too stupid to wait. So when Garber wouldn't cough up, that nasty redhead temper of yours flared up like it always does when you don't get your way. So you had a fight with him and you killed him. All because you wanted to cut ole Louie out of the goddamn action." He started advancing toward her. "Isn't that how it went, baby? All because you wanted to cut me out." His breath was coming in short gasps. "Isn't that it?" He had temporarily forgotten I was there. I started to move cautiously as he continued yelling, louder and louder, "Tell me, isn't it?" at Lucy. I was easing up off the sofa as I saw her hand slip down along the arm under the cushion. Louie's right hand with the gun cradled in it had moved up to use the piece as a club, but before I had a chance to make my move, Lucy's hand came up with a .22 gleaming in it. She shot once. Right into his heart.

In a second Louie's sneer had crumbled into disbelief and he began to pitch straight at Lucy. She put her hands up to protect herself from his falling, but at the last instant he fell off to the side. I was already up. Lucy jumped up as soon as Louie hit the sofa, the .22 aimed at me. I figured I was gone, too, but she dropped it at her side and sagged into the chair with a slight moan.

I moved and took the gun from her. There was no resistance. Her eyes were half closed and a little moan escaped at the end of each breath. I poured her a drink and waited for her to snap out of it.

"You didn't count on him remembering this place, did you?"

She shook her head. "We only came here once, before my aunt died—it was hers—and he was dead drunk. And stayed dead drunk. Spent most of his time at the bar down the road. I never figured he would find it. I've been trying to get rid of the loser for six months now. I didn't want it to happen this way." She shuddered. "He was so crazy. He showed up here tonight and he knocked me out before I had a chance to explain anything." She put a hand on her jaw. "When I came to all the lights were out and then someone—you—started banging on the window. I just wanted the whole nightmare to go away. Everything. I wished I'd never done what I did to Stan. He had been my friend." She was drained and tired and the illusion of beauty André had spoken of was trying to peep from under the cosmetics. I wondered why she'd gone wrong, but there were too many other things to think about.

"You mean the ten thousand dollars he gave you."

Her head jerked up. "How do you know?"

"The check stub is still in the check book. The police know it's there, too."

She smiled. "Not much of a crook, am I? You know, I don't think Stan really minded giving me all that money. He said he was glad to give it to me since I'd brought up his and Jeannette's little girl. I guess he felt sorry for me, too. I had gone crying to him because I was destitute even though I'd been working for twenty years, and he gave me the job and any money I ever asked for without question."

"Why did you send him that blackmail note?"

She looked puzzled. I explained. "Oh, that," she said. "I'd forgotten. Louie was responsible for that. Is it a bore or can I ask you how you know about it?"

"Garber's daughter showed it to me."

Her faced paled even under the powder. "My God. I never meant to cause that kind of trouble. How horrible. Damn Louie, anyway," She began to cry. "I'm glad I shot him."

"It was self-defense," I said. "But what about Garber?"

She shook her head vehemently. "Not Stan. I didn't do that. I've been feeling horrible since I heard. I started feeling bad about the money after I got here. I was going to give it back. The check's still in there." She indicated a closed door. "I haven't had the heart to cash it."

"The police think you killed him."

"I didn't, but what difference does it make now? I wish I were dead." Total defeat sealed the words.

For some reason, maybe the defeat, I believed her. For some reason I was sure that ballistics would show that the .22 I was holding had not been the murder weapon. "Is that story about Mrs. Garber showing up the truth?"

"Most of it," she said indifferently.

"All except that you were already packed and left with her?"

She nodded, her eyes transfixed and dreamy. "Louie was right about that much—I was trying to get away from him, but not to cut him out of the money, but because he'd gotten so violent."

"But you didn't leave town until the next day." She looked at me questioningly. "You might as well come clean now, Lucy. You'll be cleared if you didn't kill him. That check was dated Monday."

"Okay, so I was afraid Mrs. Garber would kill me. She looked like she meant business. I went to a motel that night and showed up early at the store. Stan was already there. I told him that she had visited me and that I was leaving town and asked him for the money. He wrote out the check and then the guy told me he wished me nothing but good luck. Can you believe it?"

"Did you tell him that his wife said she knew about his other daughter?"

"No, I didn't have the heart. You see, I wasn't so sure I believed her myself. I just couldn't bring it up." Her eyes filled with tears. She tried to blink them away. "I was afraid she hadn't known before. I couldn't tell him I'd told her about

Jeannette and everything just because she'd frightened it out of me. He'd been so much in love with Jeannette. But I guess if her daughter had that note, she must have known about it, too."

"No, I don't think so. I'm sure her daughter never showed her that note."

She didn't acknowledge the statement. It just didn't have the same meaning for her that it did for me.

"What kind of gun was Mrs. Garber carrying, Lucy?"

"Small, like that," she said pointing at the gun I was holding, "with a pearl handle."

I looked down at the .22. "Why didn't you believe Mrs. Garber knew about Lise André?"

"Brother, you sure know some stuff," she said. "I thought something in her face changed when I told her that I was blackmailing Stan. I could have been wrong. I was afraid of her so I went into a lot of explanation about how it all had come about. She didn't seem to be really listening after I mentioned my friendship with Jeannette, and that I had been with Lise for all those years. She seemed to get, I don't know, nervous, like I'd struck a bad chord. I thought if she did know something, she didn't know the extent to which things had gone." She stopped. Then, "You know all about those years, too, don't you? How did you get involved?"

There was no reason to tell her and I didn't want to go into it, anyway.

"Did Mrs. Garber hire you?" she pressed.

A knock at the door saved me from having to lie.

"Open up, Miss McDermott. It's the sheriff." I recognized the voice.

I went to the door, opened it and handed him the gun. Slade's eyes almost popped out of his head. Shark stood behind him, but the only expression his face knew was a contemptuous sneer.

"So sorry, Deputy," I said, "It looks like you boys are a little late for the action."

34

How to Take a Life

IT TOOK A WHILE to get everything iced down. Slade was so annoyed that I'd been in on the kill without him that he refused to let me talk to Lucy anymore that night. That was okay. What wasn't okay was the way he shoved me in a room with Shark while I gave my statement twice. Then Earl himself came in and I gave it again. And then one more time for the machine. He tried hard to pin something on me, but two hours later he decided that it was too much work, gave me my gun and told me to hit the road. He expressed hope that he wouldn't have to lay eyes on my mug twice in a lifetime. I shared the same hope.

Before facing the drive back to New Orleans I pumped myself up with a lot of coffee that never did do much to keep me awake but seemed to ease some pain.

I hit the city and drove straight to the hospital. The medicinal smells seemed especially strong and sickening as I walked through the corridors. The nurses' heads raised and their eyes flashed disapproval as I pushed through the swinging doors and walked to their station situated in the center of the circle of tiny rooms. The monitors were all lit and beeping, busily sketching the lines that gave a visual representation of the heartbeats within the rooms. I had a thought about how they couldn't show the heartaches that accompanied the beats, which was a pretty good indication of the shape I was in that morning.

A nurse who had almost the same color hair as Lucy McDermott came up to find out who I was and tell me that I had half an hour to wait before visiting hours. Her features kept getting displaced by Lucy's as she talked to me in hushed tones. I blinked a few times before I started on the importance of the visit, only I was having trouble convincing even myself. She seemed definitely unmoved. I was drawing in a breath to try another convincing aspect of my plight when a second nurse drew up to enter the conversation.

"Are you Mr. Rafferty?" she asked. I said I was. She glanced at the first nurse. "I think it will be alright," she said. "Mrs. Garber asked for you all day yesterday. She seemed quite agitated. Her daughter has been trying to locate you." I muttered that I had been out of town and she pointed at the door to Mrs. Garber's room.

I tiptoed in, leaving the door open a quarter. Mrs. Garber lay well tucked into the sheets in the narrow space between the bed rails. She was so thin that her body was indiscernible except for the rise of her feet in the bedding. Her head was sunken in a hollow of the pillow, making her face small and vulnerable. Her eyes were closed and their lids were white, with a transparent quality, like the rest of the skin on her face. She looked more dead than alive, but the monitor sent out an almost steady beep and drew thin, irregularly spaced lines while an apparatus at her nose blew oxygen into her lungs. I stood with my hands on the rail listening to the beeping and the bubbling of the oxygen. Her thin white hands with their bright blue lines lay open on the sheet. I shifted my gaze back to her face and almost immediately her eyes opened, their icy blue burning in her otherwise still face.

There were to be no preliminaries.

"You know why I wanted to see you?" she asked.

"You want to tell me that you killed your husband."

Her eyes never faltered but it took a while before she said, "Yes. But first you must tell me that you will try to protect Catherine from any further consequences of this shameful business." She spoke slowly, like she was tired, but her voice was strong—stronger than I would have expected.

"I'll do my best to keep the publicity down. I'm sure Lieutenant Rankin will help, too."

"I don't mean just the publicity. She must be spared any more pain. She has been the victim of stupid mistakes made over twenty years ago. She must not be a victim any longer. She must try to forget about it, but she is going to need help. I'm asking you because I know she has turned to you. She cares about you." She stopped and I knew she was waiting for me to say something.

"I care about her, too, Mrs. Garber."

"I needed to hear you say that. You must understand that she has not had a normal life. There is no possibility for her to have one while either her father or I live. She was a precocious child who was damaged emotionally at an early age. It has been difficult for her to have friends or be close to anyone in any way at all. Why is it that a person must be dying before realizing these things? It is a small consolation to say you did your best but my soul shall not rest in peace for having said it."

"Why did you kill him, Mrs. Garber?"

Her eyes closed and fluttered open. "Why?" she repeated bitterly. "Because he was a dishonorable man who shoved aside his wife and daughter to have an affair with a woman who was no better than a tramp." Her anger was as fresh as it would have been if it had all happened yesterday. She raised a withered hand and let it fall back to the sheets. When she spoke again it was with less anger. "I'm afraid I had possession confused with love. It hurt me terribly, and I shared every bit of that hurt and all of the reasons for it with

Catherine. She was only seven years old. That was a very great sin. I never did know the entire story, but to have it completed by that woman's friend . . ." Bitterness rose into her eyes, making them seem to burn even brighter. I knew she was trying, but she still could not separate herself emotionally from the past.

"But I must tell the story coherently, so it can be repeated to the police. They must have their facts, mustn't they? Have they found Lucy McDermott yet?"

"Yesterday."

"Have you met her?" I said I had. "A despicable woman. I couldn't understand why Stanley hired her. She belonged in a gutter, not in the bookstore. But I didn't say anything about it until I found out about all the money he had given her. I knew if I asked him about it I wouldn't get any answers. So I went directly to her. That was the day before Stanley—before I killed Stanley. I took the gun. I had assumed they were having an affair, but she denied it. I had expected her to do that, but then she told me she had known Stanley from the days of his affair with Jeannette André and that she had raised his and Jeannette's little girl. She was blackmailing him."

"You didn't know about the child?"

"No. It shocked me. I didn't really hear what else she said. I didn't need to—I knew most of it already. She agreed to leave town after I threatened her. We left together and I went home. Stanley and I had a terrible argument. Twenty years' worth of anger poured out. We were making the same mistakes all over again. He had started it all and I wouldn't let it drop. He wanted to push everything aside, forget it happened. But he kept trying to push me aside, too, just like he'd always done, to go off into his own little world where he had lived during most of our marriage. I became more and more worked up until it's a wonder I didn't drop dead that day. Catherine walked in during all that. She locked herself in her room and wouldn't come out. I know she heard every word. I knew what she was suffering and I think it was then that I decided to kill him. It was a very cold and calculated decision. I went to the store the next morning and did it."

She had become very tired while telling me her story and now her eyes closed. I stood for a moment and then started to leave, but a cold, veined hand came up and clutched mine on the bed rail. Her eyes were wet, but not as bright as they had been.

"I deserved that bullet. All these years. I wouldn't let her forget it. I talked about it. I told her every horrible thing I knew about him. I wanted her to know. I wanted to protect her. I didn't want it to ever happen to her." She paused as one side of her mouth dropped in a grimace. "I pulled that trigger twenty years ago," she said. The hand slid back to her side and the eyes closed again. I glanced up at the monitor. The beeps were coming very far apart and the jagged lines were not reaching as high as they had.

I walked stiffly to the door and jerked it open. Catherine was standing on the other side of it, one foot in the room. Her mouth was quivering and her eyes, her whole face was full of misery. I felt something that went far beyond sympathy and I desperately wanted to do something to help her, but I was helpless as a drowning kitten as she passed me on the way to her mother's side.

I went on out leaving the door open as before and stood with my back to it a few steps away. I wasn't there very long when three nurses rushed past me into the room. I turned to see a straight line on the monitor.

Outside in the waiting room I sat dragging on cigarette after cigarette like the same kitten back on the bank of the river sucking in the air.

When Catherine came through the swinging doors her eyes were blank. I sat with her and held her. She looked at me, first with disbelief, then with despair. She would put her hand on my arm, but it kept slipping off like she couldn't hold on. It was like that for a while. I wanted to take her home, but when we got down to the parking lot she told me she had to be alone and would I come in the evening. I followed her to make sure she made it alright and then went on uptown.

35

Deathbed Wish

I SLEPT for about two hours and woke with a start that almost landed me on the floor. I felt vile, but I was in a hurry to do something. I dashed around the apartment shaving, showering, and changing clothes before I realized that I didn't know what I was doing or why I was in such a damn hurry.

I ate lunch and then went up to the office and played around with the heavy assortment of junk mail that Thursdays always bring. I usually throw most of it directly into the trash can, but not that day. That day I went through every piece. If I was pressed hard I might be able to remember what some of it was about, but my mind wasn't on what I was doing. I was using it as a decoy, for something else to concentrate on instead of the small details from the past week that kept cropping up and gaining footholds in my memory. The mail wasn't nearly as stimulating.

I finally sat back with my feet on the desk and let the details swarm. I wasn't seeing the picture in its totality, just isolated vignettes juxtaposed with perfect clarity like they were being reeled off onto a screen in front of me. I saw a seven-year-old child being poisoned by a bitter marriage, helpless, having to hear and absorb all the ruinous details, like it or not. Then the same seven-year-old child, but a woman now, beautiful and withdrawn. One of André's frogs loomed into view and a white hand with large blue veins reached out to pat its head. Two people stood in a darkened room trying to touch each other, frustrated behind a barrier of long-armed demons. One of the arms reached out and clutched at the air. The picture dispersed by fragments, leaving only the arm in a circle of light. The circle broadened, encompassing Lise André as she had been that day in the farmhouse. She faded out of the spotlight and a parade of faces took their turns in it like flashbacks of the cast at the end of a movie: Al the bartender as he leaned on the bar talking to me; Carter Fleming smiling big to show his perfect squared-off teeth; Mrs. Parry with a cigarette growing from her bottom lip; a haughty Lucy as I had imagined her to be but not as I had seen her; the Boy Scout, his bulbous cheeks quaking with fury. The light went out for quite a while before Stanley Garber materialized sitting behind his desk, dead. Mrs. Garber buttoned his coat neatly, but the hand that reached for his glasses jerked back suddenly and she left them on his mouth.

For the second time that day I started. I felt shaky around the stomach. I was sweating. I was beginning to get an idea about what I should do. I wasn't sure I could. All my life I'd had this fixation about being tough. Rather, about not being tough. It was such a cliché to be a tough guy from the Channel. The way the old man talked seemed like a travesty to me. It wasn't realistic. But he would have made his decision about this one, shown his grit, the real stuff. He would have been the all-knowing hero to the end. The consequences be damned. This is what had to be done. I put a call in to Uncle Roddy.

It took him a long time to pick up and when he did it was obvious that my timing was bad.

"What do you want, Neal?" He sounded harassed and tired. "If you got trouble or any bright ideas, call back later."

"Give me a break, Uncle Roddy. I was just wondering how things are going."

"Swell. Swell." He dragged the words out.

"I take it that means Lucy McDermott isn't saying what you'd like her to say."

"We're working on it," he said.

"No go on the gun?" The old conversational stall.

"She didn't do it with that one," he snapped. I nodded like he was sitting across the desk from me. Silence grew like a fungus in the wire. "Do you know something I oughta know?" he demanded.

I was clutching the phone like it was a lifeline. "No," I said.

"Then I'll talk to you later," he said and hung up.

The phone stayed glued to my ear for a few seconds and when I put it back in its cradle, it was like I was putting an infant to bed.

The palms of my hands were moist. I wheeled around in the chair and flung open the bottom desk drawer. The bottle of bourbon wasn't there anymore.

The cicadas were out in force as I walked up the familiar path through the treed area. I think I noticed every gnarled branch. Even the dew on the grass stood out glistening in the light from the houses. I saw every crystalline detail.

All the lights in the Garber house seemed to be on. The shades were up and the curtains pulled away from the front windows. The place looked almost cheerful.

When Catherine opened the door I could still see a lot of suffering on her face, but to me she was so beautiful that I involuntarily stopped breathing. There was no gray in her eyes. They were soft and blue like that billowy edgeless blue of the sky right after a spring rain, before the sun gets too bright and turns it into a hard blue ceiling.

I put my arm around her shoulders. "Are you alright?" I asked.

She nodded and smiled weakly at me. "I guess I'm going to make it."

We went into the living room. I couldn't take my eyes off her. I ran my hand down her arm and put my fingers through hers. I led her over to the sofa. We sat very close to each other.

"Neal," she said, "there is something I want to say to you." She paused. "This week—I really may not have made it through this week, you know," her eyes filled with tears, "without you . . ."

"I know. It's okay. You don't have to say those things."

She rubbed her eyes. "But I want you to know."

"I do. Really."

I didn't want that kind of talk between us. Not yet. I had some important things to say to her first, and I didn't want the issue clouded like that. I didn't want to be diverted.

"Would you like a drink?" she asked.

"No. I'm fine."

She put her arm across me and leaned her head on me. It felt heavy, the hair up against the side of my face smooth and thick. The lights in the room seemed to dim. I closed my eyes. I thought I could feel every movement of her body against my own. I opened my eyes for a second, but closed them again because the room seemed to be leaning precariously. I felt curiously removed, like part of me had become dislodged and was far away or was viewing everything from far away. I was strangely suspended, floating, but quiet, the only still thing in a noiselessly loud flurry of movement around me. There was what seemed to be a fractional moment in which there was nothing, and then everything slipped together and Catherine and I were kissing each other. One hand was in her hair, pulling her to me so that her lips would press harder against mine. She took my hand that was straying at her waist and moved it up her satiny-feeling lounging dress to her breast. All hell broke loose in my head. I moved my hands to her shoulders and pushed away from her. Her eyes opened slowly.

"I'll take that drink now," I said.

She got up, wrapping the dress tightly across her breasts where it had gaped open. I pulled myself together and lit a cigarette. The hand that shook it from the pack was none too steady. She handed me the drink and grazed me softly as she sat back down.

"Were you in Florida looking for Lucy McDermott?" she asked. I nodded. "Did you find her?"

"Yes."

She looked at me sadly. "I guess it was all for nothing."

"No, I wouldn't say that. It satisfied my curiosity." I told her briefly what had happened, and that the police were questioning Lucy now about her father's murder.

She got nervous while I talked. "Look, Neal, I don't think I want to talk about all this right now. Let's forget about it for tonight."

"I can't," I said. I got up. "Your mother hung by a thread waiting to get rid of her guilt before she died. And she wanted to make sure that someone would take care of you when she was gone. She chose me for both those purposes."

Her eyes slitted. "You're being cruel."

"No, no I'm not, Catherine. I'm trying to handle what she told me the best way I know how."

"Have you told the police?"

"No. And I'm not going to."

"But what about Lucy McDermott? It sounds like they're trying to hang her."

"Let them try. They'll get her for blackmail. That's all."

She seemed confused. "Why aren't you just going to tell them?"

"I'd rather let them figure it out for themselves."

"But will they?" she asked quietly.

"I don't know. Maybe not. Maybe not the whole thing. I have to get it clear in my mind first." I stopped, not knowing how to go on. I took a deep breath.

"Your mother went to the bookstore, Catherine, but I don't think someone in her state of health could kill like that. Also, I don't understand why she would wait twenty years after the fact. Because Lucy McDermott was blackmailing your father? I don't think so. She took care of Lucy in her own way. What she was trying to tell me was that she symbolically pulled the trigger. She felt as guilty as if she had. But she was at the bookstore, alright. She buttoned his coat."

Catherine stared at me, frozen to her spot on the sofa. "I don't understand, Neal. What are you trying to say?"

I clenched and unclenched my hands to release some of the tension. "When we were talking the other night in the restaurant about Carter Fleming's son taking the books, I expected you to ask me how he had managed to get them. But you didn't. You didn't because you already knew. You went to the shop that morning and you heard them arguing outside in the alley. You already knew Lucy had been blackmailing your father. You had that note and a year to figure it out. And you were still angry about the quarrel you walked in on the day before, but it probably enraged you that your father would allow the son of a man who had cheated him to blackmail him with those books. You were so enraged that it never occurred to you that he was getting back at that man by allowing his own son to walk off with ninety thousand dollars' worth of his property." I stopped for breath. "Don't you see, Catherine? I didn't pick up on it the other night in the restaurant because I didn't want to."

Her face drained. The tawny, golden skin got sallow. Her eyes were huge, gray and smoky looking. "Why are you doing this?" Her voice was a thin whisper.

I went over to her. "Because this has to be straight between us." I took the fists she had balled her hands into and held them tightly. "It's very important. Do you understand?"

Her face looked like it was ready to fall apart, but she nodded and spoke haltingly, like she was forcing herself to speak. "He always pushed me away like he pushed Mother away, like he detested us both. I didn't want him to detest me. I wanted him to love me, but he always turned away. He always withdrew. He wouldn't let me in." An edge of hysteria crept into her voice. "I hated him. I hated him for it." She started to cry. "I didn't realize until he was dead how much like him I am."

She sat there and cried and I held on to her while she did. I was glad she was crying. I pushed her head down on my shoulder and I rocked her back and forth, and I was glad that she was letting it all go. I didn't stay glad for very long. As her crying subsided I felt her body, that had been relaxed up against me, get taut. I tried to keep rocking her, but she was rigid against the movement. I lifted her head. Her face was no longer torn by the deep, tugging tragedy. Composure latched onto her features and her eyes, tears drying underneath them, were blackening. I tried to get her to respond to me, but she continued to withdraw until the light froze like hard slivers of ice deep down in the bottomless pits which were no longer seeing. If there had been any choice, I would have preferred the creepy feeling I had as I stood in front of Lucy McDermott's beach house.

I watched her until I couldn't take it any longer. I got up and turned all the lights off, then went back and sat beside her. I sat there and waited. I knew then I was going to wait for a long time. I dimly heard the cicadas outside in the picture-book forest, and I thought that the moon seemed to be struggling to send its light through the trees and into the dark room, but that was no doubt a projection of my own misery. If I was having any other thought at that moment it was that I still wanted her very much.

36

Epilogue

JUST TO SHOW YOU how funny things will turn out—I learned sometime later that Lucy McDermott managed to convince the police that those sums of money from Garber had been bonuses, gifts for, as she put it, extra services. She presented the check for ten grand to Rankin and asked that it be returned, that she just couldn't have accepted that kind of money as a gift. Actually the money had never really left the family—either Catherine or Mrs. Garber had put a stop on it at the bank. Or had Garber himself?

When I called Chase Manhattan Jones to tell him that now was as good a time as any for Carter the Third to break out of hiding, he told me that Carter had served two days in purgatory at the farm house and then returned to New Orleans alone for the final judgment. Dante's hell probably looked tame compared to the scene that must have followed in the Audubon Place mansion. Chase, one of the last of the Renaissance men, was out to make his fortune in the contracting-promoting business: He would contract anything for a slice of change and in that way promoted himself. He gave me seven phone numbers where I could reach him if I ever required any service short of surgery. He was still with Lise André at the Broome Street loft. And Robert André not only finished his memoirs but got them published. I'm waiting for the movie.